BREA

Michael Symmons Roberts is the author of a novel, *Patrick's Alphabet*, and five collections of poetry, including *Corpus*, which won the 2004 Whitbread Poetry Award, and *Burning Babylon*, which was shortlisted for the T.S. Eliot Prize. He is a frequent collaborator with the composer James MacMillan and is also an award-winning radio writer and documentary film-maker.

www.symmonsroberts.com

Poetry

Soft Keys
Raising Sparks
Burning Babylon
Corpus
The Half Healed

Fiction

Patrick's Alphabet

MICHAEL SYMMONS ROBERTS

Breath

VINTAGE BOOKS
London

Published by Vintage 2009

2 4 6 8 10 9 7 5 3 1

First published in Great Britain in 2008 by
Jonathan Cape

Vintage
Random House, 20 Vauxhall Bridge Road,
London SW1V 2SA

www.vintage-books.co.uk

Addresses for companies within
The Penguin Random House Group can be found at:
global.penguinrandomhouse.com

The Random House Group Limited Reg. No. 954009

A CIP catalogue record for this book
is available from the British Library

ISBN 9780099497233

Penguin Random House is committed to a sustainable future for
our business, our readers and our planet. This book is made from
Forest Stewardship Council® certified paper.

Printed and bound in Great Britain by Clays Ltd, Elcograf S.p.A.

To Deborah, Stephen, James and William

BREATH

I

The dogs have a lot to answer for. Something needs to be done, but nobody does it. It is not a priority. The dogs are not out of control. They control themselves. The people are not their masters. Wild can be tamed, but feral knows what tame means, knows its comforts and constraints, and chooses against it.

Before the war, they were lapdogs, guide dogs, sheepdogs. Then as village turned on village, house on house, son on father, they shook off their names and found each other. Five years into the new peace, they are just dogs. Packs form and fight and reform. As the city rebuilds itself, the packs move on. Kicked out of a derelict shop or hotel, they find new wastelands to pick and piss on. Somebody must be feeding them. They are too numerous to survive on scraps from bins.

A lot of people in this city think the war veterans are to blame. Privately, they say the war vets are feeding the dogs and sheltering them at night. No one says it publicly because feelings about the war vets are too difficult, too mixed. They did, after all, go and fight for their land, for their people. But in the years since they came home, many of them slid down through cracks in the fabric: losing jobs, hitting the bottle, ending up out on the streets in makeshift settlements.

Like the dogs, the war vets are shunted from place to place as reconstruction slowly spreads. They are the guilty conscience of this once proud Southern city, a city of imperial grandeur and high culture. But apart from turning a blind eye to their thefts and fights the city does nothing for them. As for the war vets themselves, if they are ever asked they blame the North for their predicament. If the North hadn't started the war, they would still be living high on the hog in their glorious city.

After dark, a fleet of government sponsored vans sets out with guns, nets and poisons, to try to cull the dogs. The guns all have silencers, because the last thing this city wants to hear is gunfire at night.

A Tuesday. Late afternoon on a clear, sharp winter's day. Witness reports said traffic was heavy and steady. Some cars had lights on, some not. It was dusk, and drivers make their own decisions about lights. That is why dusk is dangerous, according to the police. Eyewitnesses said he was cycling at a fair pace, weaving between the cars. He seemed to be in a hurry. He found a channel between two lines of cars, and stood on the pedals to get a burst of speed. He wanted to get through on amber, to beat the lights. At the second he broke through the queues, the lights turned red, and he alone flew out across the junction. The ridgeback hit the front wheel of his bike so hard that Jamie flew a good ten feet before landing on his head in the road. One driver said that moments before the accident he saw the dog's head turn as its eyes locked on a rival pack across the road. In that instant, said the driver, he could see what was about to happen, but by the time he hit the car horn it was over. The boy lay without breathing on the tarmac, and the ridgeback – a pedigree, and once a treasured pet – was shaking a collie by the throat on the other side of the road. The rest of his pack had followed him into the attack, and they were making such a noise that only one driver got out to look at the boy. That driver was the main witness. When he felt for a pulse there was nothing definite. There was something, but he half believed it was his own pulse echoing in his fingers. A shopkeeper came out to see what the fuss was, then went back into his shop and called the police. The driver had made a full statement. The ridgeback, rare enough to be picked out in any pack, was tracked down and destroyed.

II

Control. These are his staff. This is his hospital. Control. As soon as they see you emotionally naked you've lost their respect, and once you've lost that you never get it back. Those walls are a disgrace. It's all very well having hi-tech touch-screens next to every bed but what happens when the building falls apart? *Jamie. Jamie at two or three toddling on the beach, picking up shells. Jamie.* Those walls. He thought he'd issued a written order for the corridors to be painted. He did issue an order. So why hasn't it been done? Unless it was done, and now that coat is peeling too. When was the order issued? It's years since he's been up here. He stays away from clinical areas. It's for the best. You don't want your staff to think you're spying. *Picking up shells, and holding them against his ear. Jamie at two.* Control. PLEASE WASH YOUR HANDS. Something should be done about the lighting here. It isn't adequate. On a winter's afternoon you could come a cropper. *Oh God, Jamie.* Control. If you can run a hospital you can run yourself. You can run your life. In the end, they are your staff, and you have to be professional. This is what the world does. You can try to run your life, but then a pack of dogs runs into the road. *Jamie on a bike. Jamie at two or three picking up shells. Jamie in the road. Jamie behind that door, on a bed, wired up to God knows what.* Control. Control.

The world does this. The world will punish you for settling down in it, for thinking you know the way it works. He knew that the world did this to people. But now he KNOWS it. This is the way the world ends. Not with a bang. *Is Jamie behind that door? Has he already gone? What are they doing? Why is it taking so long?* Whoever comes out of there, and whatever they say to him, control will be maintained. He will sit here for as long as it takes. Why is it so dark? This is Kristin-tide, and it should be light. So much for saints. So much for St Kristin and her dazzling festival. *Kristin and all the saints please pray for Jamie. Kristin and all the saints please pray for me.* Is that what they say? Kristin and all the saints. Where are they? Who are they? Do the saints stand in serried ranks watching us all fuck things up and not lifting a finger unless you specifically ask them? Unless you ask them by name? *Kristin please pray for Jamie.* A shut door is a wall. There is no sound from the other side. Not a hum nor a murmur. Is it the thickness of the door sealing in the sound? Or is all silent in there? Has the world lapsed into silence? Has the world gone dark at Kristin-tide? Can the world not hear the siren in his heart? *Dark. Dark. O God. Our help. In ages. Past. O God.* St Kristin. Can a name have power? How about St Lucy? How about using her Northern name? St Lucy, yes. Perhaps the saint prefers her Northern name, and favours prayers sent to that address? How ridiculous. How utterly fucking ridiculous. *Jamie at three picking up shells . . .*

'Sir.'

The door is still shut, but a doctor is standing next to him.

'Mr Andrews, sir.'

The voice is soft, but Andrews doesn't want to hear it. The doctor must have come round the corner. Why didn't he come through that door? Why didn't the man come through the big silent door that he's been hitting with prayers and pleas?

'Sorry, I was miles away.'

'I'm sorry, sir, but I do have some news about your son . . .'

'Jamie.'

'Yes, the news on Jamie. There is no easy way of saying this . . .'

'You don't need to say it. I knew as soon as I came in.'

He can't remember the doctor's name. He knew it once, because he knew everyone's name. He issued all their contracts. He interviewed most of them when they applied for their jobs. He could go up to his office now and find out how much that doctor is paid, where he trained, any disciplinary issues, everything. But just now his name has gone.

'I'm sorry.'

The doctor dips his head, as if in prayer. It doesn't look right. It looks phoney. People who are really sorry don't dip their heads like that. Andrews wants rid of him.

'Thank you. There's no need for this. I know all about the bedside manner courses. I probably sent you on one. That's enough, thank you. Now leave me to it.'

The doctor looks hurt, but tries to hide it. He nods and says sorry again before hurrying away. Andrews stands for a moment in the corridor. What does he do now? Who is he now? Not a father any longer. A bereaved father? So does he go home? *Oh God. Jamie.* He remembers a family holiday, when he still had a family. Jamie was about two or three and he was wandering along the beach stopping every now and then to pick up shells. He was so caught up in his world that he wandered away, two or three hundred yards away from his parents. Then he suddenly looked up and howled. He had lost his bearings and looked the wrong way for his parents. All he could see was a vast, empty shore and the sea crashing onto it.

Andrews is standing in a corridor of his own hospital, outside a room in which his dead son lies. He can't seem to move, but he can't just stand here. He's still the hospital administrator. Manager. Executive. Chief. What does he do now? What do people do when this happens to them? He'll go back to the office and do some work.

At his office door, his PA looks anxious.

'Any news of Jamie?'

'It's not good.'

For a moment, she looks as if she wants to comfort him, but he walks past and into his office, closing the door behind him. Work. Work will be the answer. Work can save the world, can save a life. If he loses himself in his work, he will find a way forward. *The Way Forward . . .*

He wakes up his computer and finds the document open in front of him. It is a very important piece of work. Crucial. He has been drafting and redrafting for weeks, but the hardest part keeps coming back to haunt him: the war, old enmities, deep-seated hatreds. How can this be managed in a modern workplace? He is the man. His is the beacon trust, the exemplar hospital, the one to show *The Way Forward*. The cursor blinks mid-sentence, just where he'd left it. Some things are constant. He is a senior executive. He has work to do. He has a mission statement to complete: *The Way Forward – Strategies for Integration and Cooperation in Modern Healthcare.* He rests his fingers on the keyboard. *Section Three: The Challenge of Sectarianism.* The cursor vanishes and reappears repeatedly after the word *'history'*. He reads back over the paragraph:

Effective recruitment and retention can be compromised by a failure to address this issue. Although existing anti-discrimination policies are producing more equitable structures in many of our hospitals, there is a need for ongoing training and appraisal to ensure that we move forward together, nationally and regionally. Through effective management of this issue, staff can take ownership of their own future, as stakeholders in an integrated healthcare system. Far from an attempt to deny our recent history

He stares at the cursor: on off on off on off on off. He types a comma and the words *'this is . . .'* but the sentence resists completion. He reads the paragraph again, but cannot make sense of it. Concentration. He holds his head still in his hands, and starts to read again. But there's no sanctuary here. A knock on the door and it's opened by a woman in a business suit. She's peering in, staring at him, looking awkward.

'Geoff, I'm so sorry.'

'I'd like to be left alone please, Karla.'

'There are things I need to discuss with you.'

'It's hardly the time.'

'About Jamie.'

'Whatever it is, it can wait.'

She comes in anyway, quietly pulling the door shut behind her. He stands up from his desk and turns his back on her, looking out of his window. His hands are in his pockets. Outside, there are rows of cars and rows of trees. It all looks very neat. It was worth the spend – whatever the arguments – to give the hospital an orderly appearance from outside. He is proud of the landscaping. Presentation is part of *The Way Forward*.

One moment he is gazing out across rows of young pine and spruce, the next he is on his knees and gasping for breath between sobs.

'Come on, Geoff. Sit down.'

She helps him up and sits him on the sofa. She sits next to him with her arm around his shoulders. His head is buried in his hands. After a few minutes, he regains enough composure to speak.

'Thank you. I'm glad you came. Can you leave me now, please?'

She doesn't move, just keeps holding him and shushes him like a baby. He moves away from her and stands up.

'Karla, we need to keep this on a professional level. We agreed.'

'We did. We will.'

'So why are you here?'

'I'm here on a professional level, Geoff. I'm duty counsellor today, and you are a bereaved parent.'

'Oh please . . .'

He gets up and brushes his jacket, straightens his tie. She gets up too, and walks across to him, putting her arm around him again.

'Don't touch me.'

She takes her arm away, steps away from him, and folds her arms.

'You appointed me, remember.'

'Not to counsel *me*, I didn't.'

'You're not making this easy.'

'Easy for whom?'

He opens a desk drawer and takes out a cigar. He lights it and ostentatiously blows smoke in her direction. Opportunities for rebellion are few and far between in his life. Responsibilities crowd them out. To smoke a fat cigar in a hospital is as far as it goes these days. Not much of a rebellion, but his office is just down the corridor from the lung transplant unit, so there's always the chance that a faint whiff of tobacco will find its way down there. Karla decides to ignore the cigar.

'Geoff, there is an issue to discuss.'

'What issue? My son has died in an accident. Is that the "issue"?'

The smoke is pungent, and far from sweet. It's a dry, rather old cigar he had been saving for a celebration. He didn't know what the celebration would be, but he felt it was important to mark significant events. He spent too much of his life in the future. The present was just something to get through on the way there. It had its urgencies, its challenges, even its satisfactions as work was done, but it rarely amounted to pleasure. About a year ago he felt his life was racing by and he decided to anchor it with tiny weights, details, private rituals to mark the passing of this or that. When he bought the cigar he had in mind completing the annual appraisals, or signing off next year's budget. He didn't have in mind the passing of his only child.

'The issue is transplantation. Donor organs.'

'I see.'

He hadn't seen it coming. It had never crossed his mind. As soon as she said it, it was obvious.

'Jamie is in a state of brainstem death, but most of his other organs are still in good condition. There is an opportunity to save life here through transplantation. But we need your permission as the next of kin.'

He stubs out the cigar in an empty coffee cup, and snaps back at her.

'Bit predatory, isn't it? Do you always prey on the bereaved like this?'

'Please, Geoff. You know there is a narrow window of opportunity. Jamie didn't carry a donor card, but many people don't. It doesn't mean they're against the idea. It is accepted in such cases that we can make an early enquiry of the next of kin. You run this hospital, so you know better than anyone the importance of donor organs and the reputation of this hospital for providing and receiving them.'

'Have you finished?'

He turns his back on her to look out of his window again. A very light rain has drifted in from the sea, washing the cars and making the leaves shine on the trees. On another day, in another life, it might be beautiful, but not today.

'Geoff?'

All he can see in his mind's eye is an image of his son, lying in the middle of a busy city street, with his bike in twists and bits around him, and his head broken on the road. Was it rain like this, was it this very rain that made the road slick and gave his tyres less purchase? Was it cold enough for the rain to freeze a little as it touched the road? Did the dog hit him with a glancing blow, and would he have saved himself if his bike hadn't slid from under him?

'Geoff?'

Was it meteorology? Just a natural confluence of temperatures, levels of humidity, landscape and pressure combining to produce a shower of rain little thicker than a mist? If that shower was playing a role in the death of his son in one street, and perking up the leaves of a window box in the next, then the world was insane. It was insane or random. Either way, his emotional response to it as something purposeful, predictable, was nothing short of madness.

'Geoff. I need an answer.'

'Okay, okay. Do it. But not the eyes. Leave his eyes.'

She looks into his. She can see they are pinched and moist. It is a long time since she has looked into his eyes. These days, she avoids them and it's only their voices that meet. She wants to put her arms around him, but that would cross a line. The line of professionalism is all that protects them from each other. She has to ask the professional question.

'Is there something wrong with his eyes? A problem?'

'His eyes are perfect. Were perfect. I just don't want them taken.'

'Okay. That's fine. I don't think it's the eyes they need.'

'What is it?'

'Lungs.'

'Okay. That's fine. Thank you.'

He turns back to face the window. She walks away, wondering why he would single out the eyes to bury with his son. The heart she could understand, but why the eyes? Bereavement changes the way people think. They make irrational judgements, and it's her job to help them through that. In this case, she decides there's nothing more to say. Perhaps he wants his son to have vision, to see what's in front of him when he wakes up on the other side. Perhaps he fears he won't recognise his son in the next world without those eyes. Perhaps he just sees Jamie's eyes each time he shuts his own, and cannot bear the thought of them being cut out. Sometimes working in medicine can disable you, can stifle you with too much knowledge, too much detail.

'Karla.'

She is about to shut the door behind her. 'I'd like to see him, one last time. Complete. Before they take anything.'

'Are you sure?'

'Quite sure.'

'I'll arrange it.'

A Civil War in Nine Cigarettes:

1

The one lit by a new father in the waiting room of a hospital maternity unit after witnessing the birth of his first and only child. He was struck by the boy's blue-black head of hair – no bald baby this – and his near-translucent skin as smooth as his mother's. He stepped outside while the midwives weighed and checked him over. He hadn't prayed for years, but he lit a cigarette like incense to help him.

It was the middle of the night. The unit was full of babies: sleeping, crying, feeding, some still kicking to be born. But none of the other babies looked like his. This boy was a Northern boy. The shuffle of the gene-pack between Southern father and Northern mother had produced a baby from the mountains.

'Good luck to him. No. More than that. Not just good luck, not chance. Take care of him, O Lord. Take care of this son of the mountains as he grows up in this city on the plains.'

Each week, each month, each year more ravens, kites and crows were swooping from the peaks to scavenge on the streets. They came in search of carrion, but there was none. Their senses had misled them. Either that or their senses were so keen that they perceived a feast before it came.

III

It is mid-evening when the call comes. Jude was hoping it would come later. Night standby means all through the night, but the later the call comes, the more chance that the flight will take place after dawn. A mid-evening call means flying through the small hours, and that is not her best time. But the calls come when the calls come, and you have to make a rational choice. She likes the difficulty, the responsibility. She is still a new enough pilot to be thrilled at being trusted. They offer her a flight, and she is the one with the knowledge to weigh up weather, distance, route, time and fuel. She is the one who must decide.

She makes a coffee and spreads out the maps on the table. It's a long way. Good for the flying hours, but a long flight at night. Her sister says she should go for it. Her sister is always encouraging her.

'This is your chance Jude. A big night flight. Grab it! I'll come with you!'

Her sister is not here. Her sister has been missing for months. Missing presumed lost. Presumed dead by some. But she still talks inside Jude's head. No one else knows that she hears her sister's voice. They wouldn't understand.

She hears the door go and her husband comes in. He brings the cold in with him. He is a bear of a man and with a drink inside him he seems to fill the kitchen as he tries to walk across it in a straight line. Her sister can't stand him.

'Oh, God. He's back.'

He opens the fridge and starts taking things out.

'Got a call then, babe?'

'Agency says it's a lung.'

'A lung? Shame. If it was a liver you could bring it home. We've got some onions . . .'

'Not funny.'

He cuts some bread, shifting her maps aside to make room on the kitchen table. She folds the maps to give him space.

'Where you taking this lung?'

'Long way. A hospital up North.'

He stops slicing the bread, and comes round to look at the map over her shoulder.

'North of the border?'

'There isn't a border any more, Tom.'

'Like hell there isn't.'

He goes back to the bread, piling up sliced meat on it. He keeps looking up at her, but she is saying nothing. She is looking at her maps and not catching his eye. After a few minutes, she folds the maps, picks up the cordless phone and heads for the door. Her sister is chanting in her head.

'Leave him, leave him, leave him, leave him . . .'

'You're not doing it, are you?'

'Yes, Tom, I'm going.'

'You can't go there.'

'It's a medical flight. I'm a professional pilot. I fly where the work is.'

'And betray your own people?'

She leaves the room, and he follows her, catching her in the hallway dialling a number. He takes the phone off her and puts it in his pocket.

'Do you know where I've been tonight, Jude?'

Her sister knows.

'He's been drinking.'

'Drinking? Give me the phone back.'

She reaches towards his pocket but he grabs her wrist.

'Not drinking. A crisis meeting. All the reconstruction money's going North. All of it. They're getting new homes, new hospitals, flash hotels. What are we getting, eh? What's coming here? The time has come, Jude . . .'

'Tom. There is no North and South any more. It's over.'

'It's not over. It's just starting. We're talking about direct action . . .'

Jude stares at him. Her voice is quiet but firm.

'Who were you meeting?'

'You know who he was meeting.'

Tom ignores the question.

'One of our war vets died in hospital this morning. Did you know that? He died because he refused to accept the capitulation. Every week when he went to pick up his army pension he would stand in the street and swallow the coins. He would only stop when they put those bastards on trial for what they did. But the trial never happened, and he swallowed so many that he couldn't eat.'

'I said, who were you meeting?'

He looks down, then up at his wife. He rolls up his sleeve and reveals a fresh, roughly-shaped tattoo of a fist on his forearm. She looks at it and turns away in disgust.

'Give me the phone. I've got to go.'

'It's resistance, Jude. I'm proud to be part of it, and you should be proud of me too.'

'No. You're wrong. There's nothing to resist. You have become . . .'

Her words tail off. Her sister's don't.

'. . . *a monster, a terrorist, a victim* . . .'

She looks at him, this man she married, with his paramilitary tattoo and his glazed eyes and his lost hopes.

'Are you going to let me make this call?'

She pulls her wrist free from him, but his hand goes into his pocket and clutches the phone. He stares at her, waiting for her to give way. She looks down, but he quietly taps the glass of a picture on the wall beside them. It's a picture of Jude's father in military uniform. She grabs her coat from a hook on the wall, opens the door and leaves. As the door slams, Tom takes the phone out of his pocket and throws it at the door, shattering a glass panel.

IV

They asked him to wait, and he's good at that. It is a gift that comes with age. His grandchildren do not have it. Neither does his daughter. He is alone in the waiting room except for a young nurse on a stepladder, hanging baubles on a Christmas tree. The TV in the corner is screening a baseball game from another continent. He doesn't know the rules, so he watches the tree instead. Apart from the TV, the room is elegant and old world, with its antique leather sofas and a side table with a marble bust in the centre. Every minute or so, he takes an alarm clock out of his baggy jacket's inside pocket and checks the time.

'That's not exactly a pocket watch.'

The nurse has come down the ladder and is smiling at him.

'A present from my daughter.'

'Lovely. A bit big though.'

'I don't like digits . . . Prefer hands . . . This has digits.'

He can manage a few words at a time, before dragging at the air to recover his breath. Every couple of minutes he presses a mask to his face and takes a mouthful of oxygen from a cylinder on a trolley beside him. Other people his age wheel trolleys of shopping or their chattels behind them. He has to wheel an off-board lung to help his weak lung cope. For years, the right lung has carried its weaker twin, has done the work of both, but now the left lung is giving up the ghost, and the right lung is not strong enough to do all the work. He puts the clock back inside his jacket, and buttons it up. If the clock had hands, it would tick, and he would like to feel the ticking under his jacket, close to his heart, to remind him of his daughter, to keep him alive.

'Are you okay? Can I get you anything?'

The nurse sits down next to him, taking a break from her work on the tree. She tilts her head to one side and smiles. He looks as small as a frail child to her, buttoned into his best suit for a wedding or funeral. She feels young and strong in his presence. He says nothing, so she tries again.

'Shall I open a window? It's a bit airless in here.'

He shakes his head.

'Too cold.'

'Have you been waiting long?'

He nods, takes out his clock and moves his finger across the face to show that he's been waiting half an hour.

'Let me see if I can speed things up for you. What's your name, sir?'

'Baras.'

'I won't be long, Mr Baras.'

She leaves the room, pausing by the door to flick a switch and turn the tree lights on. Left alone with the baseball commentary, he picks up a remote control from the table in front of him. He presses a button and the sound climbs to a deafening pitch. He fumbles with the control and hits the big red button in the top corner. The TV dies instantly and he notices, in the sudden still of the room, that the alarm on his clock is softly beeping. He takes it out of his pocket, and stares at it as if to make it tell him why it's ringing. He switches it off, and notices that the tree is flashing, not in a regular pattern but flickering. The nurse has wrapped loops and loops of white lights around it, and they are all on the blink.

Between the lights, the tree is full of eyes, some enamelled in peacock colours, some in delicate glass, some drawn by children on bits of card and hung up with string. It's a tree full of eyes in honour of a saint. Baras is not interested in saints. What he knows about Saint Lucy is that she had her throat cut, and she's associated with light, with vision. He doesn't know when or where she lived, or whether she lived at all. He knows that her myth and symbols are stamped onto the face of this mountainous northern nation like a brand. He knows that people love her, and the weaker minded ask her for help. He sees himself, even in old age, as sharp-minded and clear-sighted, and those faculties convince him that the people's love of their saint is best left alone.

He doesn't like being stared at, even if it is just a tree doing the staring, so he hauls himself to his feet and shuffles across to the window. He wheels his oxygen cylinder with him. It takes a lot of breath to get there, but he leans on the ledge with both hands and looks out. The hospital is set among bare trees, but this is a high window, and he looks over spindle branches onto a medieval roofscape.

The narrow streets of this spa town are buzzing with jewellers, confectioners, shoe shops and galleries, but from up here, where none of the detail is visible, it could be full of peasants hauling beasts to market. This latticework of ancient roofs survived the war untouched. It was not too protected to be bombed, just too irrelevant. The Southern planes and rockets had been trained on more suburban, populous parts of the city, places where the impact would be wide and deep, where seeds of despair could be sown.

Now, as dusk falls, the lights are coming on across the city, the Lucy lights, the night's eyes, along and across the narrow streets like a net. Beyond the roofs, higher than the window, higher than the sun, great mountains bank against the sky.

'I think I've got things moving now, sir.'

Baras turns and manages a half-smile.

'Was I forgotten?'

'Not forgotten. They were just preparing your room. They're sorry to keep you waiting.'

She props the door open with her foot, and wheels in an elegant-looking basket chair.

'To save your breath, sir.'

She helps him down into the chair, and wheels him out of the waiting room towards the lift. He carries the oxygen tank across his knee.

'Like a hotel,' he says, as the lift door closes, but his voice is weak and the nurse doesn't hear him.

'A hotel,' he repeats to himself.

If the hospital is like a hotel, then this must be the bridal suite. Baras is wheeled into an opulent room with a round polished table in the centre. On the table is a vase of white flowers, and high above the flowers is a crystal chandelier. There are folded news-papers on the table, a glass bowl piled high with fruit, a telephone and a silver bowl with a large shell in it. The shell looks like a skull.

'Make yourself at home. Can I get you a tea or coffee?'

'Tea. Please. Weak.'

The nurse leaves, and Baras tries to cross the room, pushing down on the wheel rims of the chair. His arms aren't strong enough, so he gets out of the chair and walks, slowly, using the table, a bookcase, the drinks trolley – yes, a drinks trolley full of spirits – for support. If you are going to die, this is not a bad place to do it. The bay window looks out across a lake and mountains: the living room is beautifully furnished. The bathroom is immaculate in marble, brass and folded white cotton. The bedroom is fit for a seduction, four-poster and all. But he is not going to die here. He is here to be reborn.

He notices his suitcase on the bed, sits down and unclips it. Inside is his other suit, cut from thick, dark green tweed and silk. It was handmade in the moun-tains by strong quiet people, Northern people, his people. Many great men have climbed mountains in suits like this one. He plans to wear it when he leaves, but it must be hung up. He lifts it out and takes it to the wardrobe. He opens the wardrobe door and drops the suit. This is not a wardrobe. It is another room. It is windowless, lit only by the spilt light from the bedroom and the faint glow of red and green lights on digital displays.

Baras feels for a light switch, and finds one. Great banks of fluorescent light shudder into life and the room is revealed. White tiled walls close in on a central table, with more lights arching over it. Racks of instruments surround the bed. It is sterile, dazzling, sharp. It looks like a hotel kitchen, with surfaces scoured clean every night. A huge freezer shivers in the corner. Baras knows at once that no fish is filleted here, no vegetables are chopped on that table. This room is for meat, and the meat is him.

'Has someone left the lights on in there?' The nurse puts a cup of tea down on the bedside table.

'I dropped my suit . . .'

'Oh, okay. I'll deal with it . . .'

She steps past him, turns the lights out, and shuts the door, offering an arm to help him back towards the bed.

'The doctor will come and see you soon. Drink some tea and try to relax. There are things he needs to discuss with you.'

She picks up his suit off the floor, brushes it down with her hand and takes it to the wardrobe on the other side of the room.

The room has changed for him now. For all its chateau elegance, for all the drapes and beeswaxed wood and trinkets, this is nothing but an ante-chamber. As soon as the steel and tile heart is revealed, this old-world style feels as fake and thin as a *trompe l'œil*.

He lies back on the bed, takes a couple of drags from the oxygen tank and listens to his breath slipping out and back, out and back, out and back. Are his lungs pulling and pushing the air, or is the air working him like an old pair of bellows? Out and back, out and back, out and back. Lord Jesus Christ Son of God / have mercy on me a sinner, Lord Jesus Christ Son of God / have mercy on me a sinner, Lord Jesus Christ Son of God / have mercy on me a sinner. After fifty years, the Jesus Prayer is there, under his breath where it was supposed to be. It was put there at school, an implant sewn into the fabric of breath and intended to last him a lifetime.

Lord Jesus Christ Son of God with the out breath, *have mercy on me a sinner* with the in. *Lord Jesus Christ Son of God / have mercy on me a sinner, Lord Jesus Christ Son of God / have mercy on me a sinner.* In the holiest men and women, the greatest saints, the prayer and the breath would grow inseparable, indistinguishable. To be alive was to be in a state of prayer and penitence. That is what they told him. That is what they taught the children.

Baras has no interest in saints, nor in the Jesus Prayer. It might as well be 'Heartbreak Hotel' or 'Ten Green Bottles'. It is an old song stuck in the memory of an old man, annoyingly persistent, but relaxing like a lullaby or nursery rhyme – yes – he could almost sleep.

A Civil War in Nine Cigarettes:

2

The one taken to pieces by a prisoner in a previous war, who had used the white cigarette paper as a parchment, and written a poem of love to his wife, to his people, to his land. Then he reassembled the cigarette and had it smuggled to his wife as a secret token of their love and their hopes for the future.

When he survived and came home, his people adopted it as a symbol of their strength and resilience. The poem was reproduced across the nation, framed on bedroom walls, blown up to poster size in schoolrooms.

Three decades later the nation once again began to tear itself apart. As the border closed and battle lines were drawn, he saw an opportunity. He was an older man now, a wiser one. He knew he could exploit the cigarette poem, and his fame for writing it.

Soon he had become a member of the ruling elite. More than that, a talisman. That tiny poem – about ice and birds, about his wife and mountains and colossal northern skies – had given him the power of life and death. He could command men to do whatever he wanted. It was utterly intoxicating.

He never wrote another poem.

V

Andrews is a model employer. He never asks his staff about their war record. He has trained himself to be accent deaf. Okay, not accent deaf, but accent neutral. Of course, he hears it. How could he not hear the rasp of that dialect? Even when they work for years down here, they never lose that Northern burr. He hears it, but he has taught himself to tune away from it, to see a man for a man, a woman for a woman.

Effective recruitment and retention can be compromised by a failure to address this issue.

His hospital has a good scattering of accents, and some of his senior staff have roots in the mountains. He does, sometimes, wonder what secrets they hold, but he believes in the amnesty, in the conspiracy of silence. If we open those doors again, no one will be able to close them.

Although existing anti-discrimination policies are producing more equitable structures in many of our hospitals, there is a need for ongoing training and appraisal to ensure that we move forward together, nationally and regionally.

Except of course, they never closed at all. You can declare an armistice, but you can't impose a peace, not a deep peace of the heart. The details snag like seeds on your sleeves or trouser legs. In a couple of decades, some newspaper will do a straw poll on the city streets and no one will know what the war was for, no one will remember why it started or ended. Facts like those will be locked up in the universities. But the details will stick in the throat for generations.

What people will remember is that women were raped in the streets in front of their own children, raped by men who may now serve them in shops, wait on them in restaurants. They will remember that one Northern warlord had the eyes of every prisoner in his camp – men, women and children – cut out with kitchen knives. Why did he do it? Some said it was his insurance against the future. He knew that neither side could win, and that some sort of treaty would be brokered. They also said that foreign governments would try to press for war crimes trials, and that blind victims would find it hard to identify the man who ran the camp. Others said he kept a freezer full of eyes in his house, dried and hardened like humbugs, that he used them to decorate his house on their national day, in honour of their patron saint. They were his spoils of war.

Somehow, it all comes back to Andrews now, as he walks down the corridors of his own hospital to take a last look at the body of his only son. It all comes back, even though he knows that his son's death was an accident. The dogs would not be on the streets if there had not been a war, and the war would not have happened if it had not been for them.

Through effective management, staff can take ownership of their own future, as stakeholders in an integrated healthcare system. Far from an attempt to deny our recent history

Now he can see, as clear as war paint, the pale sun-starved skins of his Northern staff members. As he walks through groups of doctors, nurses, porters, he can pick out the Northerners with barely a glance. He can hear every tongue-turn of their accents. One of them is waiting for him as he reaches the door of the theatre. Even before she opens her mouth, her origins are clear from her blue-black hair and her gaunt face. Her skin is so thin he thinks if he shone a torch in her face he could map every vein in her head. He even catches himself, fleetingly, imagining her pale-paper breasts. He was always attracted to Northern women.

'Are you sure you want to go in, sir?'

She looks genuinely concerned, not just going through the handbook on 'dealing with bereaved parents'. He reaches out a hand and touches her hand, but leaves it there a few seconds too long, and she gently pulls it away.

'I'm sorry, I . . .'

'Don't worry, sir. It's up to you. I just wanted to make sure you were fully prepared to go in there.'

'I'm okay. Yes. Thank you. I know what to expect.'

She opens the door and stands aside so he can walk

in. She offers to stay with him, but he says he would rather be alone. Alone with his son. Alone with Jamie.

Jamie is a shape under a white sheet, a landscape of fell slopes and peaks. Only his face is uncovered, and his eyes have been closed. Andrews takes one corner of the sheet and keeps on slowly pulling until the landscape of his son is fully revealed. Naked without its shroud, Jamie's body is still warm, still wired up to a life support machine. There is no life, no hope of life, but the machine keeps the blood in motion, keeps the vital organs fed. The machine will not be switched off until the lung has been removed.

Why now, when he wants to say goodbye to his son the man? Why now has Jamie become a child again? Andrews focuses on the strong jaw, the stubble around the chin. This is a young man, but the harder he looks, the more Andrews sees his son as a boy.

It had taken him a whole week to get Jamie cycling. At that time, when Jamie was about seven, he and his wife had decided to give their boy a taste of the seaside. They had rented a cabin on the coast, and hired bikes to explore the back roads and causeways linking the mainland to a string of tidal islands.

Long afternoons he would run alongside the bike as Jamie wobbled and zigzagged down the roads. Then he started taking him down to the beach in the evening, when the tide was out and the sand was vast, untrodden and still firm enough to take a bike. If Jamie fell off, as he often did, the sand would soften his fall. In the evenings, the low sun picked out an intricate tracery of tread marks like lace, with a flourish wherever he had fallen off.

By the end of the week, Jamie was racing his parents on bikes across the causeways, cutting it fine to beat the tides back from the islands. He had such a look of joy and such a rush of confidence once he could ride the thing. As soon as they got back to the city, they bought him a bike. He had taken a few bruises from the hard sand, but it was worth it, because now he was free.

A few bruises. Like these. Only these are more than a few. His body is much bigger now than when he was seven, so the bruises will be bigger too. The bruises and the cuts. His body. Oh, God. Is it still his body? Is he still there? Is he in it? Andrews realises, looking down at the body of his son, how little he knew that body. He knew, of course, the face and hands, and in summer he saw the arms and legs, but he had not really seen this body since his son reached his teens. Seeing it now, the body of a young man, he is seized at once by pride and despair. Here is the handsome, beautiful boy he made, the baby he held in utter calm in the moments after his birth. He gently lifts the eyelids to see one last time those brown eyes, speckled like marbled eggs, moist and pin-sharp in life, but utterly empty now. He remembers his wife relating – at almost every birthday throughout Jamie's child-hood – how she woke up in her hospital bed the night after he was born, and looked across to see two huge brown eyes staring at her through the bars of his cot next to her bed. She said he was not crying, not desperate or worried, just quietly astonished by it all, taking the measure of his new world.

Now Andrews is struck by the stillness of the body

of his son, its beauty and its unnatural, perfect calm, way beyond sleep, beyond any possibility of life. Yet the body seems so plausible too, as if one small wire has worked a little loose, and a few seconds' work could reanimate the whole thing. Despite the cuts on the legs, Jamie's face and upper torso are unblemished. They say it was a head injury that killed the boy, but there's no visible trace of it. Perhaps it's on the back of the head. Maybe he will see it if he lifts the head and looks underneath. He leans across and puts a hand on each side of the head as if to lift it, but finds himself kissing the boy on the forehead instead.

The nurse comes back, so quietly he doesn't hear the door.

'Are you all right, sir?'

He thinks she has seen the kiss, and worries for a moment that it undermines his authority, his profes-sionalism.

'I'm fine, thank you.'

He pulls his shirt cuffs out of his jacket sleeves, straightening himself.

'Only, the team is waiting to come in.'

'The team?'

'The transplant team, sir.'

'Ah.'

'They don't want to rush you.'

'They're not rushing me. I'm finished.'

The nurse stands by the door but bows her head and stares at her shoes, in case he wants a last, private moment with the body of his son. But he isn't looking at his son. He's looking at her.

'Can I stay?'

He speaks quickly, as if he can't quite believe what he's asking.

'Stay?'

'Yes. Can I stay and watch them work on him?'

She looks up, and sees him for the first time as a grieving parent.

'I don't think you really want to do that.'

'No. You're right.'

She puts an arm around him, and gently leads him away from the body of his son, out of the room and into the corridor, where a surgical team is killing time discussing last night's TV. He thanks the nurse for her sensitivity, then he heads back to his office. But he cannot get out of his head the thought that now the blade is going in, now the tight skin of his chest is folded open like a wing, now the cage door of the ribs is prised open to get at the treasures inside. He cannot help imagining the strong young heart, trembling on a steel plate, and the lungs still warm and full of breath. He wonders if the lungs have stored the last breaths of the dead boy, like a print on the retina. Could they hold his last words somewhere, like a voicemail in breath, lost among the alveoli, the countless tributaries of lung?

He stops in the corridor outside his office, suddenly sure that he should go back down, should burst into the theatre before the lung is cut out, and call them all to silence. He should place a hand on the lung and gently press it, pushing out the last breaths. He should lean in and smell the scent of the city, the streets, the ghost of coffee or whisky, and maybe, just maybe, he would catch a whisper of a word or two, a last word from son to father.

He stands still for what feels like minutes. Then he sits down at the end of a row of four chairs kept in the corridor for waiting visitors. On the coffee table next to him is a pile of well-thumbed magazines. The one on the top has a singer he's never heard of standing in front of a white mansion with the caption 'Come and see my dream home.' For the second time today he feels himself breaking down. He curls up on the chairs as if they were a bed, and shuts his eyes.

VI

It is about keeping warm. That's what this stage is about. Get the engine running and the heaters on full while you wait. Don't worry about all the rest. Trust your routine.

Jude tries to trust her routine, but normally she is not alone. Usually there is someone there to help her remember. For most night flights in the past she had a trainer with her. Once you become a solo pilot, you have to ring round the list of trainees who will fly for the experience. They are supposed to keep you company, and to help you stay awake on the long trips. It is another mind on board to make sure you get the routine right.

Tonight will be her first solo night flight. When Tom threw the phone at the front door after her, she thought of going back and picking it up, but it didn't seem worth the row. She drove around the corner, then she called the agency on her mobile to accept the job. She also rang round the list of trainees, but they were all busy.

So she came in on her own to a dark corner of the airport, and let herself into the office. She had done more map work and weather checks, opened up the hangar, towed the plane out, gone through the routine. Checks. All lights working. No oil leaks.

De-ice the wings. The leather seats were cold when she first climbed in. The windscreen was so chilled her breath condensed as it hit the glass. She had locked the hangar, switched on the heating, and waited for the car to come.

Waiting and waiting. Will they ever come? Did Tom pick up the phone and call the agency to turn down the flight on her behalf? No. Not possible. She spoke to the agency and fixed it up. Her sister thinks he would though, the voice of her sister obsessing about Tom inside her head.

'He's trying to stop you. Doesn't like you flying. Leave him Jude. He's no good. He's a bad man, Jude . . .'

Jude listens to her sister's pleas, but she doesn't reply. At least, not out loud. Her sister's voice is not a real voice. Jude knows that, but knowing it doesn't make the voice any easier to ignore. At first, it was the odd word screamed out in the middle of the night: '*Help*', or '*Jude*', or '*Rescue me*'. It began about a month after Jess had disappeared. Sleepwalking, Jess used to call it, claiming to remember nothing of her walks in the dark. But Jude didn't buy it. Jude always thought her sister was awake. Wandering the city streets one night six months ago, she never wandered back. It was in the papers for a few days – MISSING SLEEPWALKER NEW SIGHTINGS – but no trace of Jess showed up. It was when the papers dropped the story that the voice began to speak inside her head. Her husband called it grief, but it felt more like a consolation. Tom had asked her about it again a week later and she said the voice had stopped. In fact it had grown more insistent. After the initial shouts and screams it settled to a lower pitch and now for months her sister has been with her as she works, rests, sleeps.

What is the delay here? Why has no one come to meet her, to hand over the cargo? Must be a medical hold-up, or maybe the car has crashed on its way to the airport. Surely not. Maybe the body doesn't want to give up its lung? She wouldn't be surprised. Lungs and eyes are what the world needs now. The future is about what you say and what you see. Never mind what you hear or what you touch. Orators and eye-witnesses, givers of orders and impartial observers. In time of peace you don't need the men with steaming hearts. The hearts are what got us into this trouble in the first place. Now put the hearts into storage, put the passions and the pain and the crimson into cold storage. Bring out the lungs to give apologies, words of hope and reconciliation, words of direction. Then bring the eyes to make sure there's a vision behind the words, to make sure the words turn into actions.

Perhaps this lung came from a peacemaker. Maybe he felt he had much more to say and didn't want to give it up. Perhaps just as the doctors were trying to cut it out of him, his ribcage was closing on their hands like a trap.

Warm warm warm. The plane is getting comfortable. She turns the heating off again. She wishes the controls were subtler. On a long night flight the temperature is crucial. She must be warm enough to fly without shivering, but not so warm as to drift into sleep over the mountains. When will the car arrive? Maybe her husband was right. She should have turned it down. Not for his reasons but because she's tired, and the flight is too long and the night is too dark. He was right for all the wrong reasons. And for that reason alone she has to make the flight. She thinks of Tom at home: drinking, fuming, cursing. What is he doing to the house? To her things? She runs through the things she would miss: the clothes, the photographs, her father's watch and chain, her mother's locket with its tiny perfect pearl of sea-glass picked up on a distant shore when she was still a girl, and treasured ever since. She thinks of all these things in turn and lets them go. He can do what he wants.

'That's right, Jude. Let him go. He's no good. He's no good. Let him go . . .'

She is on a life or death mission. She is working at the edge of those two now, the place where they touch. Where do the dead go when they are done with us? After the war, everyone knew someone who had passed away, crossed the line. She knows the dead don't go far. They stick around, but most of us no longer see them. They even speak, if anyone will listen. She thinks of them as radio. She thinks of them a lot.

A Civil War in Nine Cigarettes:

3

The Turkish filterless smoked by a long-dead man glimpsed across the street by his great-grandson. How did his great-grandson recognise him? From photographs, stories, from the archaic cut of his jacket, from his tall hat. In the end, he just knew. He looked into that face and knew it was his own blood coursing behind it.

The long dead man was smoking outside an undertaker's office, as if he had climbed out of a coffin and stepped outside to wake himself up with a cigarette. His great-grandson watched him from across the street. They made eye contact but neither said a word. When the long dead man finished his smoke he threw the fag end down and stubbed it out with his boot. Then he walked off round the corner.

His great-grandson rushed over as the apparition vanished, and found the stub was still there in the road. He picked it up and it was warm. He blew on it, smelt it. It was the real thing. He put it in his pocket and wondered if he was insane. He wondered if it was a case of mistaken identity, but there was something about the look the man had given him that made him discount that.

That same night, a rocket attack took out the undertaker's office and the buildings on either side of it.

VII

Baras is surprised to wake up. Or rather, surprised to have been asleep. These days when he sleeps it is a thin state. He cannot draw the deep breaths that lead to full, rich slumber. Somehow, here of all places, he wakes up feeling like a traveller who has cut much further into the forest than ever before, into the darkest places, and come back more alive than ever.

The nurse is gently fussing around him, clearing away tea cups and plumping up pillows. She is talking about the cold outside, how she had to scrape her car windscreen this morning on her way in, how she could see even the red mountains so clearly as she drove up to the hospital. He listens, but does not respond. Her conversation is a kind of smokescreen, he thinks, to blur the fact that she is moving from maid or wait-ress to nurse, from tea cups to a cuff around his arm to take his blood pressure. She enters the numbers into a hand-held device, then packs away the kit into a small bag.

'Professor Ross will be here in a minute.'

'Who?'

'You haven't met him?'

Baras shakes his head. Professor Ross, she explains, is the man he has been waiting for, the man who will give him a new lung, the man who will give him his breath back. The way she paints him, he is a genius, a miracle-worker, a world-renowned master of the transplant arts.

'You must be an important man, Mr Baras, to have Ross himself fly up to do your transplant.'

'Ah, no. Just an old man . . .'

He pauses in mid-sentence, and she smiles sympathetically as he gathers his breath.

'. . . who is running . . . out of steam.'

She fusses and tidies some more, then leaves the room, promising to come back in a minute with a glass of water for him. But she must have been called to somebody more critical, or sidetracked into other errands because he lies on the bed for what seems like half an hour, with nothing but the shuffling of footsteps in the corridor to break the silence. He wonders about getting up to switch the TV on, but he can't quite bring himself to make the move. Eventually, the door opens and a man walks in. He is wearing a dark chalk-striped suit and a silk tie. He does not look like an international transplant expert. He looks like a stockbroker. He looks like a man who has something to sell.

'Sitting here in silence? You've got a TV over there, you know.'

'Didn't want to get up.'

'There's a remote control by your bed there.'

'Not to worry.'

Ross introduces himself, but stares out of the window as he talks, almost with his back to Baras, who finds this rude and a little unsettling. The nurse's over-zealous bedside manner may be too much, but he would like a little eye-to-eye contact with the man who is going to cut his chest open. Ross stands and stares out of the window across the mountains for what feels like minutes. The silence is uncomfortable, but Baras feels he cannot break it. Is it a prayer? Is the surgeon gathering his powers before the operation? Eventually, he steps away from the window, pulls up a chair and sits by the side of Baras' bed.

'There are some things I have to tell you. About the operation. I'm sure you're aware that there are risks.'

'I can imagine.'

'Well, I'm afraid I have to run through them anyway. There is a risk that you will not survive the operation. It is a significant risk. Even if the operation is successful, that is not the end of the risk. There is a serious possibility that your body will reject the new lung. We will put you on a regime of immuno-suppressive drugs to try to prevent that, but those drugs carry risks of their own. They can lay you open to other forms of illness.'

Now his eyes are locked on to Baras' eyes. But he sees no kindness in them. They are clear and cold. Baras takes a draught from the oxygen cylinder beside his bed.

'The records say you are sixty years old, Mr Baras. Is that right?'

'Yes.'

'Then you are right at the top of the age range for an operation like this. All these risks will be enhanced. The one advantage you have is that we're not doing a double lung transplant. Your right lung is still up to the job, I gather?'

Baras nods weakly. If he was not so tired, so breathless, so lacking in the will to respond, he might challenge these questions, this information. Surely it is not necessary to take him through all these scenarios of doom. He knows what he is here for. He is not a fool. He knows that a lung transplant is not like having a tooth pulled. There is no need to tell him all this, but Ross seems to think there is. It is standard procedure. Well, fine. But it seems like more than that. Ross seems to be enjoying the telling.

'Once your immune system is suppressed, you have an increased risk of a number of other conditions. Then there is a significant risk of infection.'

'Why are you telling me?'

'It's my job to tell you, Mr Baras. I cannot proceed without your informed consent.'

Baras stares at him, at this professor who dresses like a stockbroker, with his Southern vowels as round as pearls, his tanned face and his unblinking eyes.

'Well, you have it.'

Ross gets up, moves the chair back to the side of the room, and returns to the window with his back to the patient.

'Very well. Good. We will need to do further tests in the next hour or so, but you can assume we will operate tonight. The donor lung is on its way.'

'Where from?'

Ross turns and stares briefly at Baras. Then he sniffs and walks towards the door.

'I cannot tell you anything about the donor. Not without the consent of the family and a lot of form filling. Anyway, why do you ask?'

Baras shrugs uncomfortably. He did not warm to Ross before, but the conversation has a distinct edge now.

'You do not get to choose the donor of your lung, Mr Baras. Only God does that. You see, they have to die first. We do not arrange that part.'

Baras shuts his eyes. He wants Ross to leave. He does not need this. All he asked was where the donor came from. It was a simple question. Ross opens the door, but pauses, staring at his feet for a moment.

'I think I can tell you, without crossing any professional lines, that your donor comes from a city south of the border. More than that would be a breach of confidentiality.'

With that, Ross shoots one last glance at Baras and leaves the room. Baras doesn't see the glance, because his eyes are shut, but he hears the words.

VIII

Five more minutes and she will call the hospital. She has done everything on her list, and in double-quick time. With a transplant flight you have a duty of care, and that includes the avoidance of delay. If this flight arrives too late tonight it will not be her fault. Where is the car? If something has gone wrong with the operation, if the whole thing has been called off, then they should let the pilot know. Here she is – a trained professional – sitting wasting time at the edge of the airport, waiting for a lung.

She is about to make the call when she sees two points of light in the distance. She watches them grow and sees the dark shape of a car appear behind them. She turns the engine off, and waits until the car has stopped. It flicks its lights twice and she climbs out of the plane. The passenger in the car gets out and walks along the runway apron. She meets him halfway.

'You're late,' she says. 'What happened?'

The delivery man is not looking at her: he is looking at the sheet of paper in his hand. As he reads it, his warm breath rises like smoke into the chill night air.

'Are you Jude?'

The delivery man looks the pilot up and down.

'I thought Jude was a man's name?'

'Did you?'

'There's that Jude who's an actor . . .'

'Well this one's a pilot. Can we get on with this?'

He smirks at her.

'All right, all right.'

She doesn't flinch. She holds her hand out to receive what he has brought for her. She stares at him and wants to say, 'How many pilot hours do you have?' 'How much do you wish you could fly this plane and not spend the night delivering bits of bodies by car?' But she doesn't say any of that. She just stares, and waits for him to hand it over. He's a small man, dressed in the overalls of an ambulance driver or a paramedic, but he doesn't even drive. He just delivers.

'It's a lung tonight.'

'I know.'

She takes the handle of the plastic cool box, but the delivery boy doesn't let it go. He wants to talk.

'Going up North are you?'

She doesn't answer, but he carries on.

'Rumour is it was a teenage boy. Jimmy something or other. Son of the hospital boss, so they're all really cut up about it. Came off his bike on the corner, you know down by the . . .'

'Just give it to me.'

He has now moved beyond irritating into downright unprofessional. The way he is talking, you would think the blue cool box held a picnic, not a transplant lung.

'Okay, lady. Just being civil.'

His driver is getting impatient too and flashes the lights a couple more times. The delivery boy lets go of the cool box and Jude takes it. Immediately, she's struck by its weight. On her transplant flights as a trainee the passengers were livers and kidneys, both much lighter in their boxes. There must be a lot of ice in this one. You would think a lung would be weightless, like a balloon, almost floating on its own breath.

'D'you want to take one of these?'

The delivery boy has taken a packet of cigarettes out of his pocket and is offering them to Jude. He nods towards the lung in the box.

'. . . just in case he fancies a drag while you're up there.'

She turns and strides back towards the plane. He laughs. He shouts after her that it was only a joke, that she should lighten up. But she feels far from light.

'I'll report you in the morning.'

She puts the box on the floor behind her seat. It's so heavy that she thinks its weight will hold it steady. She switches on the radio and suddenly her isolation in the plane is broken. She's part of a network now. Air traffic controllers are talking to her. This is the real deal. They know she's on a mission, a medical emergency, so they give her priority. She taxis into position for take off. She asks air traffic for their latest on the weather and they say it looks clear. They tell her she can go in three minutes. Suddenly, she worries that the box might fall over and spill its precious cargo. Maybe it wasn't as heavy as she thought. She unstraps herself and moves the box, placing it on the seat beside her. Then she straps the box in and straps herself in.

Glancing across, it could almost be a co-pilot, belted in and facing duplicate controls to her own. She puts a hand on the lid and it feels warm. All the cold is kept inside, which is the way it should be. The heating is warming up the plane, but the lung will be safe. It will be safe with her.

'How many souls on board?'

The routine pre-flight question from air traffic suddenly rocks her. She finds herself uncertain what to say.

'Two.'

'Two?'

'Pilot and one other.'

'Is that you and me, Jude? Two souls?'

She doesn't reply to the voice of her sister. Not out loud anyway. She wants the voice to be quiet now.

'Okay, you're cleared for take off.'

Jude taxis the plane towards the runway, and as she does so she can hear the lung in its box on the seat next to hers whispering, whispering.

IX

'Mr Baras, I'm sorry to disturb you. Were you asleep?'

'No. Resting.'

'D'you mind if I come in?'

She is a thin, pale woman dressed in an ankle-length black cassock. She smiles at him as she pulls up a chair and sits by his bed.

'My name is Pascale. I'm here to visit the patients who are waiting for operations, and to see if I can help.'

'With what?'

Baras is tired, and doesn't want a conversation. But he is also anxious after the conversation with the surgeon and doesn't want to be left in silence on his own. He props himself up on the pillows and looks at her.

'Are you a priest?'

She smiles.

'I'm a minister, yes. Is there anything you'd like to talk about, or pray about?'

'You're very young.'

'Good of you to say so. Not that young, actually.'

She has cropped black hair and dark eyes. He can barely see the pupils. She seems patient, genuine. He decides she can stay. He would like her to stay for a while.

'Do I call you Mother?'

'You can call me Pascale.'

'I am not a . . . man of faith, Pascale.'

'I didn't ask if you were, Mr Baras.'

He looks around the room and sees on the large table in the centre of the room a marble chess set. He points to it.

'Will you play . . . chess with me?'

'I can't, I'm afraid. Never learned the rules.'

'Never learnt chess?'

'Sorry.'

'What did they teach you?'

'Lots of things. My parents were carnies. They toured the mountain villages with tricks and turns. You'd be surprised what I can do.'

Her face lights up as she talks about her family. Her eyes are clear, open, unguarded. With eyes like that, he thinks, she could witness the worst that the world has to show her and still look unblemished. Innocence is not a moral gift, it is a genetic quirk. Baras has seen it before and envied it. His own eyes are dimmed, tarnished by what they have taken in. Sometimes he sees them in the mirror as two lumps of frosted sea-glass, turned and turned in the tide until they lose the gift of clarity.

'Show me a trick.'

She gets up and walks across to the table in the middle of the room. She takes two of the large marble chessmen from the board and throws them from hand to hand. Then without breaking the looping cycle of the throws, she snatches a third off the board, then a fourth, until five pieces are circling between her hands.

Baras is mesmerised, but it sets him on edge. He's waiting for the smack of marble on marble as a king and queen clash in mid air and shatter on the floor.

'Careful!'

The minister smiles and, without breaking the rhythm of the throws, she picks the pieces one by one out of the air and puts them back on the table. Then she tidies them into their ranks on the chessboard and comes back to sit by his bed.

'So you see, my parents taught me something.'

They sit in silence. Baras is fiddling with a button on his cuff, undoing and doing it up, undoing, and doing. He is looking out into the room, but not at the minister. She waits for a few minutes, then clears her throat.

'Would you like me to go, Mr Baras? Would you rather be on your own?'

'No. Stay.'

She nods and waits. She is not a novice, but these situations are far from intuitive for her yet. She thinks of her training in counselling, the books she has read on pastoral work. Wait, and they will tell you what they want to tell you. Wait, and they will give. All you have to do is listen. Attend. But she waits, and he says nothing. He just looks into the room and fiddles with the button on his cuff.

'Mr Baras. Is there something you'd like to talk about?'

He shifts around on his pillows and faces her. She sees for the first time real fear in his eyes, and she panics. She tries to keep the panic locked up, not to show it in her face or in her voice, but she suddenly has no idea what she will say to this terrified man old enough to be her grandfather. Trust the training. Trust the Spirit. It will come. The words will come.

'Father . . . Mother . . .'

'Just Pascale, please.'

'Pascale . . . do you know the surgeon?'

'Professor Ross?'

'That's him.'

Suddenly she sees a clear line of conversation open up before her, a straight path of reassurance she can offer.

'I don't know him, but the staff here are very excited. He's the greatest transplant surgeon in the country, perhaps in the world they say. He doesn't normally work here. He has come up to operate on you. You are in the best possible hands, Mr Baras. You must be a very important man.'

'A retired engineer . . . That's all . . . Roads and bridges.'

'Well we certainly need bridge builders, Mr Baras.'

She smiles at him. This is going well. She can do this. But he looks away again, and starts messing with the button on his cuff.

'That man Ross has come a long way.'

'Yes, he's flown here for you.'

'He's not from the mountains.'

'No, he's not.'

The minister shifts in her seat. Now she is at sea again. She can sense where this is going, and she doesn't want to go there. She gathers her thoughts for a minute, then pitches back in. Breath or no breath, if he has something to say then he should say it.

'What's the problem, Mr Baras?'

'A Southerner.'

'Professor Ross is a Southerner, Mr Baras. Yes. I believe so.'

'Not one of us.'

Baras stares at her. She is tempted to play dumb, to pretend that geography was her weak subject. Geography and history, that is. But they both know what he means. She decides – whatever the pastoral books might say – that this is a moment to speak, not just to listen.

'The war is over, Mr Baras. I think you should be grateful to be treated by such an eminent surgeon. If I was having a lung transplant, I wouldn't care where the surgeon came from, just how good he is.'

'And the lung . . . Southern too.'

The minister gets up, as if to leave. Baras apologises, takes a few drags on the oxygen mask, blames it all on the stress of the operation. He pleads with her to stay. She sits back down, but her eyes have lost their gentleness. He has forfeited the right to be listened to. Now there are things she must say, and he must listen.

'I don't recognise the term "one of us". It is a dangerous term, a term that has led to the deaths of countless people on both sides of a stupid civil war. I will sit with you and talk, Mr Baras, but I will not entertain that kind of language.'

'Okay, okay . . . I'm sorry.'

She fetches the chess set from the table and sets it up on the edge of his bed.

'Will you teach me to play?'

'It's a long game . . . Are you sure?'

'I'm in no rush. No one wants to talk to a minister tonight. The hospital's full of atheists.'

'I'm an atheist. I told you.'

'I don't believe that for a minute.'

A Civil War in Nine Cigarettes:

4

The one offered to a villager caught in a gas attack when his wife begged for help. As he coughed and retched and battled for his breath, his desperate young wife knelt down in front of one of the enemy soldiers walking through the village. The soldier was wearing a scarf tied round his nose and mouth to protect him from lingering traces of the gas. She pleaded and pointed to her husband, hawking and wheezing, collapsed at the side of the road among a scattering of bodies. She told the soldiers of their children, of what a good father her husband was, of how she couldn't cope if he should die.

The soldier listened, then reached into his pocket, pulled out a soft pack of army issue cigarettes and offered her one to give to her husband. The other soldiers laughed. He threw the packet in her face and walked past her down the street.

X

Jude is flying the small plane by hand and eye above the river heading north, following its bends and straights. She tries to stay focused on the route, on the flight, but her thoughts keep drifting back to the boy whose lung rides in the seat next to her, the boy called Jimmy. She pictures the teenager who woke up this morning full of energy and ideas for his day, the one who now lies in the hospital morgue with his chest peeled open like a fig.

How fragile it is. All of it. How desperate that all those hopes and fears and hours of work and worry from his parents could have come to this, a lung in a picnic box. The more she thinks about him, the more she starts to choke up. She cannot cry. She has a job to do. A job and a duty. But the more she thinks about Jimmy, the louder his lung whispers from the box next to her. The lung is gibbering, scared or still in shock. Jimmy's lung, the keeper of his breath now torn from its moorings, split from its twin, naked, cold, alone.

*Dark dark the dogs do bark cold cold and ever so old
come back to me don't leave me not like this not now
o long time coming o long time going love me love me
I'll be there I'll be there for you if you'll be there for*

me dark dark love me save me by the skin of my teeth
by the love of my life by the treetops and tips of the
tenterhooks and dream songs o lily livered long legged

This is not her sister's voice. She tuned out of that voice while she did her job. This is the voice of the lung in the box. She knows it is the voice of her own thoughts, her own imagination. But she knows it is the boy's voice too. She cannot let this get to her. Lots of people hear voices. At least this voice is harmless, friendly, even vulnerable. The poor thing. The poor boy. He sounds so young, so scared. So Jude begins to sing to calm him down, to calm herself down. She sings snatches of nursery rhymes, folk songs, pop songs. But they are all snatches, because she doesn't know all the words to any of them.

She is playing the facts over and over in her head as the plane maps the river's course: the boy, the crash, the grieving, the missed opportunities, the lost hope. She banks the plane to the right, off the course of the river. As the glass tilts, she can see her home city below her.

She dips lower over the suburbs and the strings of Kristin lights between the houses shiver into focus. Beyond the houses, the city centre stands on the flood plain of its once great river. The city still has some pride, though damaged. At night the gaps are stark, dark holes in the cloak of light that a city spreads out for those that fly over it. All cities have gaps in their cloaks, but in healthy cities the gaps are parks, urban woodlands, lakes. In a wounded city like this one, the gaps are piles of rubble, wasteland where once stood hotels or office blocks or schools. Although she knows the facts, she is still rendered speechless, breathless, when she sees the damage. Until you get up here, you cannot comprehend how this city suffered under Northern guns and rockets: the destruction of the White Palace, the shattering of Martyrs' Square, the wreckage of the Hall of Heroes. She takes it all in again. And running through it all, the river sclerotic with debris: stone, steel and glass from fallen buildings. She levels the plane and the lung speaks.

My listless endless worthless loss my emptiness my good my god my cooked goose my politics my refuseniks my parcels my battles my figure hugging my despair my last three wishes my mother my father my river my endeavour my whatever

This is not like her sister's voice. Her sister will fall silent if Jude tells her, or if she needs to concentrate. This voice keeps on talking. Maybe it isn't her imagination. Maybe this is the vestigial voice of the boy, a residue of his voice lodged in his lung. It makes sense. A lung contains breath, and breath contains words, fragments of speech that are trapped, lodged in the byways and backwaters. Now, before the lung is planted in another chest, filled up with another person's breath, another person's language, before any of that takes place, the lung must clear itself of all that Jimmy had to say.

She tries to guess which part of the city he came from. If he was the son of a hospital manager it must have been one of the better suburbs. Banner Hill?

Broken Cross? Yes, Banner Hill feels right, and it's en route. She swings left and follows the north road out of the city centre. As she sees the spire of Banner Hill Church, she glances across at the cool box and recalls a conversation with an older pilot when she was training. He told her that once – on a long transplant flight at night – he had given in to the temptation to look inside the box. Everyone wants to, he said, every pilot wants to have a look, but most of the time you resist the temptation. That night he ran out of resistance, and he knew – since it was packed in ice – that a quick glance would do no harm. He had looked at the heart, and it was fine, he said. He zipped it back up and now someone is walking around with that very heart pumping inside them. No problem. Curiosity satisfied and no harm done.

Jude glances across at the box. She so badly wants to look at this lung, to see what or who she's carrying through the night. Just a look. Just the briefest of glances. Her eyes flit between the instruments in front of her and the box beside her.

Home from home stone on stone broken bones and open wounds bustle and muscle and castles in the air blessings and pressings and buildings and bedding and feeding and folding and loathing and loving and diving and weaving and moving and saving

His voice is a little louder now, reaching beyond a whisper into low, clear speech. She leaves it. She leaves well alone. She focuses on the flight because that is her job. The city is petering out below her. She pulls the plane back towards the river and picks up the main route north. This is familiar territory. During the war they were desperate to train pilots for supply runs. She would run up the river to the front line, to the border, delivering men, weapons, food. Most of those emergency pilots gave up the whole thing at the end of the war, but not Jude. She was hooked, addicted to flight. Her husband tried to talk her out of it, but he could see he was wasting his breath.

The river looks clear and sharp now she is outside the city. It's the same river, but it looks like a new one, freshly cut, so unclouded that the fish could see her thousands of feet up. But this river is heading for the damned and ruined one. This water – born of mountains, raised on moorlands, fed through caves – is heading for the city. This water will be threaded through drowned cars, across submerged girders, guns, mixed with oil and ordure. By the time it meets the sea this water may be bearing bodies: ten jumpers a week, they say, from different bridges. Jude pictures her sister Jess face down in the river, then tries to overwrite that image with the one she longs for: Jess found fast asleep but fine and well, still wandering the streets after six months of sleepwalking, sleep-eating, sleep-subsistence. They would bring her home and gently wake her up.

Suddenly she wishes – more than anything – that she had found a trainee to come up with her tonight. They would help her to keep her mind on the aircraft, not on the land below her. A trainee would keep her focused, but there isn't one. It is just her. Just her and the lung. Just her and the boy. Just her and Jimmy.

The river does look stunning, a jagged silver scar across the deep green and purple of the fields and woods. She bites her lip and looks ahead.

Wishing well animal family salary missing me lessons in mystery passion for history blackberry elders and builders and wonders and water walled gardens palaces wild places faces race against the clock by the book round the block soaked to the skin I'm in

XI

Karla stands still and breathes deeply. This is where she earns her money. This is where it bites. She kneels down in the hospital corridor and puts a hand on the shoulder of her boss, who is never governed by emotions, who insisted they could still work at the same hospital when they broke up, who is the consummate professional, who is curled up tonight like a lost child on the waiting room chairs outside his office.

'Geoff. Geoff.'

He sobs quietly and she strokes his hair.

'Come on, Geoff. It's late. You should go home. There's no point in staying here.'

He sits up slowly and wipes away his tears on the sleeves of his suit. As he looks down the too familiar corridor outside his office, the office where he has spent each weekday for the last fifteen years, he sees a row of people looking at him. His father is first in line, dressed in his butcher's overall as if he's just nipped out of the shop for a smoke. His mother is next, wiping her hands on her apron. Third to sixth in line are his grandparents on both sides, looking like characters from a period drama, with their cloth caps and pocket watches. Behind them, fading into the distance beyond the fire doors are his ancestors, tapping out clay pipes, coughing, one or two wiping their own tears away. They are all looking at him, not with bitterness or accusation, but with a quiet pity.

'Shall I get you a taxi?'

'I'm fine, Karla. I'll be all right.'

He takes her hand and holds it between his. He closes his eyes, and when he opens them his ancestors are still there, still watching him. He lifts Karla's hand and kisses it. He thanks her, and says he'll walk home. The night air will be good.

'Geoff. I'm really sorry, but there's some official stuff I need to ask you.'

'What stuff?'

'About Jamie.'

'You knew Jamie.'

'But you're the parent. I have to ask you.'

Andrews looks up to see his mother whispering something in his grandmother's ear, and his grandmother shaking her head.

'I have to ask you some questions about Jamie's lifestyle. I have to ask about drugs and sexual history.'

'For the transplant.'

'That's it.'

'Well, he smoked the odd joint, as you know.'

'But no IV drugs. No needles.'

'Karla, do we have to go through all this?'

'Okay, no needles. And his sexual history was, well, the usual.'

'The usual, I guess. He didn't tell me about it.'

'That's fine. That's it.'

She puts her arms around him and holds him, which makes him feel better and worse.

'Oh God, Karla. I don't know what to do.'

'Go home, Geoff. That's the best thing.'

She takes her arms from around him and stands up. He stands up too, then he walks over and locks his office door.

'You should be proud, Geoff. Tonight he's going to give someone else a new life. That's quite a legacy. Someone will draw breath tonight because of Jamie.'

Andrews nods, and walks down the corridor, wiping his eyes on his sleeves again, in case anyone catches sight of him and notices his tears. As he walks along the row of ancestors he wishes they would hold him, or say something to change things, but they don't. They move their heads as he walks past, watching him with kindness, but without help. They are no help at all.

He bursts through the fire doors and down the stairs to the ground floor. The main corridor is quiet out of visiting hours. He looks behind to see if the ancestors are following him, but the corridor is empty. He passes the signs to the various wards and units, and – as is his custom – translates them in his head into layman's terms. In those terms, the basic elements of life are signposted from this corridor: birth, breath, piss, shit, pulse, death. But it isn't enough. It simply isn't enough.

XII

Realising that she has let the plane drift too high, Jude pulls it down until she can see the surface of the river again. She is trying to concentrate on the flight, trying to be a good pilot. She is a good pilot. But it's hard to fly straight with the lung on the seat next to you emptying every vestige of its voice into your head.

Back later back sooner back before dark back before the lights come on the lights the lights the home fires back without a shadow back safe and sound and light and ground and sure and strong

Below the plane, the moonlit river is banking sharply to the right, and disappearing into woodland. This is the point where she must switch from river to railway. The river heads off to the sea, diverted by the higher ground, but the railway powers on, drives north up the spine of the nation. She banks to the left, but the railway is harder to locate. She takes the plane lower and, just as she is starting to panic, she sees a train. The train has five carriages, but number three is dark. This is how things are now. In a restaurant half the menu will be struck out because the ingredients are scarce. In a hotel half the rooms will be unavailable because the damage has not been repaired. In a car, people club together and drive as slowly as they can because fuel is so expensive. This is what the war has done. As if to remind us all of what has been lost, what has been damaged, every train seems to carry one dead, cold, dark carriage. And people still sit in it, because they still need to travel, and sometimes because it suits their mood to huddle in the icy darkness.

Sing sing sing are you listening can you hear me I can't breathe it's cold it's cold comfort calling and calling out over the clouds like a sower seeding rain it's all too soon it's all so soon so songless

Should she open the zip? Should she take a quick look? After all, the lung is packed in ice so there's no risk of damage. If it was critical not to open the lid, the medics would have locked it down. But it isn't locked at all, just clipped shut like a picnic.

Yet she knows the rules: you take the box, secure it firmly in the plane, fly swiftly and safely and deliver this piece of a person into the hands of the agent at the other end. She knows that none of this includes making it comfortable, tampering with the zip. But then, no one warned her that a lung would sing, would hum, would talk. Hearts don't flutter in their cool boxes. Livers don't shout the odds like old drunks. They just sit in their ice like lumps of offal. No one warned her that a lung would be so different.

See you later I'll be back before dark before the light begins to fail before it falls I'll ride on the pavement I'll keep both hands on the handlebars I won't stop

*until I get there and I won't look back I won't fall
off I won't get a flat tyre and fall I'll be back before
nightfall*

She shakes her head, fast, as if to rid it of some
wooziness, to bring it back to focus. What madness
is this? What is she playing at? She stares ahead. This
is serious business. She is on a mercy mission, medical
emergency. She has worked hard to get here. A
commercial licence. Flying for money. Now she is
flying with the big guys. Another six months of
medical flights and her hours will be up there. Once
her hours are up there, she can go for the airline jobs,
the passenger flights. That is what it's all about. And
all she has to do is to hold things together and get
this cool box safely to its destination. She is a professional. She can do this.

She sings aloud, not to the lung, but to mask any
sound its voice might be making. For all she knows,
it could be whimpering in its box, but she doesn't
want to hear it. As she sings, she sees the landscape
open up below. Small towns start to appear. Clusters
of lights on the great plains of darkness. When she
started flying, in the first months of the war, these
plains were full of lights. There were small towns and
villages, farms and hamlets everywhere. But as more
and more of them were bombed, rocketed, mortared
and abandoned, the lights became more sparse. After
the armistice, the cities were first to be rebuilt, but
what became of the people of these towns and villages?
Are they still there, sitting in the darkness, working
by candlelight until the government can get some

power back to them? Have they all fled to the cities? Sure, there are more people in her neck of the woods than before, more bedsits and house-shares, but not that many, not enough to swallow up the population of these provinces.

The radio squawks a weather warning further north. She shivers. She thought these calm skies were too good to be true. For the moment though, all ahead looks clear. She is singing a song for Kristin-tide, a song about the saint as a young girl lost in the forest, rescued by birds and taught to watch, to see, taught to have the vision of a falcon. The girl grows up able to look into a stranger's eyes and to read their thoughts, their doubts, their prayers and pain. It is one of her favourite songs from childhood, but she can't remember all the words. As she stumbles through it, the boy on the seat next to her starts to hum. Accept it. That's it. She is not going to pretend she can't hear the voice in her head because she can, and that voice knows all the words that she has forgotten.

XIII

'What's wrong with that?'

'They can't jump.'

'You said knights can jump, so why can't these?'

'Knights have horses.'

'Okay, so bishops have to walk do they?'

'. . . in diagonal lines.'

'But no jumps. Right. I get it.'

The minister gets it, but she doesn't really like it. The game seems empty, legalistic and strategic. She cannot see its appeal, but if it's helping this old man face the biggest challenge of his life, then it's a part of her ministry. She tries to imagine what it must feel like to know that within hours someone you have barely met will cut you open, take out one of your lungs and put a lung from a stranger in its place. Is he terrified? He seems anxious, but not terrified. Maybe the ability to stop short of terror comes with age. Maybe he's had enough of labouring for breath and is happy to risk it all for a new lease of life.

'I can win . . . in three moves.'

'What? Already? I've only just learned what the bishops do.'

'Three moves.'

She has always loathed hospitals. She hated them even before she saw her father die in one, just days before the ceasefire. It was a desperate place, a desperate time. What demonic turn of mind would make an army step up its assault in the last days of the war? Why would you not wind down, but rather push every gun, rocket and plane as hard as you could until the bell rings, until peace begins? They said the Southern generals wanted victory, not peace, and tried to clutch one from the jaws of the other. They said lots of things about the Southern generals, and she tried to treat those things with caution and forgiveness.

'And . . . three.'

'Is that it?'

'Checkmate.'

For a woman who hates hospitals, this was an unwise career choice. Except that it wasn't a choice at all. She had always thought that vocations were a process of gentle persuasion: recurrent thoughts, repeated conversations, a growing awareness that this is the path you are meant to walk. But hers wasn't like that. Her call was so persistent that she couldn't escape it. By the time she was ordained, she felt like Jonah in the belly of the whale. Running away was no longer an option. She said *yes* to get some peace.

Since then, she has clocked up hours in hospitals. But this is different. It is not like other hospitals. Converted from a spa once used by kaisers, kings and tsars, it looks more like a mountain palace, with its copper domes and arched windows. This is not just the finest hospital north of the border, it is the finest in the whole country. Pastoral duties here certainly beat treading the wards in the average district general.

So plush are the rooms that she can almost forget what happens here. Almost.

'Another game?'

'No, thank you. I'd only lose again.'

Baras smiles and rests his head back on the pillows. She arranges the pieces on the board as best she can, then lifts it carefully across to the table. When she comes back to sit by the bed he is fingering the button on his cuff again.

'Shall I go now? Would you like to get some sleep?'

'No. Stay.'

'Shall I read to you?'

'No. I want to talk.'

The minister settles herself, crossing her legs and sitting up straight, trying to look receptive, interested, hoping that whatever he says, she will think of something helpful to say back.

'What would you like to talk about?'

'Absolution.'

'Absolution?'

He nods, but doesn't catch her eye. She blows gently through her lips, as if to blow a candle out. She tries to remember what to say. Of course he wants absolution. He thinks he could die tonight, and he's right to think that. He wants to set his soul in order.

'Okay. Absolution. It's not a word we use much these days. We tend to talk more about reconciliation. It's about coming to terms with things we've done, expressing them to God, and asking for his forgiveness. Essentially it's about rebalancing your relationship with your creator.'

'For me . . . it's absolution.'

'Well, I can't just give it to you. It isn't mine to

give. You have to go through confession to God and asking for forgiveness.'

'You can't . . . absolve me?'

'Only God can absolve you. I can be a vehicle for your confession, I can help you talk it through, but in the end it's down to you and God.'

Baras closes his eyes, and his head slumps forward as if he's used up what little energy he had. She feels the moment calls for some greater gesture of love and support. She reaches across and puts a hand on his arm. He doesn't flinch. He doesn't move a muscle. He just lies there, breathing deeply, digging deep for every breath. She tries again.

'Would you like to talk it through with me?'

'You are . . . very young.'

'Does that matter?'

'Help me sit up.'

She reaches behind him and puts her hands under his arms. With a shared effort he shifts up higher on his pillows, until he is sitting upright. For the first time since the chess game, he looks her in the eyes.

'Okay.'

She smiles and sits back. Low key is the way. Don't put him off. Help him through this with gentle encouragement. Help him to say what he needs to say. He seems uncomfortable. His face tightens. He looks away from her as he begins his confession.

'There were . . . women.'

She feels like saying 'How many?', 'When?', 'Did your wife know?' but she knows she can't say any of that. She looks at him as blankly as she can – attentive but supportive. But it doesn't matter anyway, because he is not looking at her. He is looking across the room, out of the window.

'It was long ago.'

'Okay.'

She nods. He turns to look at her again.

'Will you . . . absolve me now?'

'Well, Mr Baras. If you've made your peace with God, and come to terms with what you've done, then you already have forgiveness. You don't need some form of words from me to make it happen.'

'I do . . . Please say them.'

'You must find the words yourself, Mr Baras.'

'I'm no poet.'

'Would you rather talk it through a little more? It sometimes helps if you can explore your own emotions, your motivations, to try to understand why you did what you did, and how you learned from that.'

He closes his eyes and his head seems to sink into the pillow, as if an invisible hand is pushing it down. The minister is lost. She is far out at sea. The script she was following in her head now seems obsolete. She asks him if he is okay, but the answer seems so obvious that she feels stupid asking him. He doesn't answer. After what feels like minutes, she takes his hand between hers and prays.

'O Lord, I pray that Mr Baras will find true peace. Please help him to move on from the mistakes of the past, and to experience the fullness of your love and forgiveness. Amen.'

She opens her eyes, but his remain closed. She stands up and explains that she will move on now, that since he clearly wants to be alone, she will leave him. Just as she is wondering if he has lost consciousness, he opens his eyes and looks at her.

'Don't go.'

'There are other people I can see. If you'd like to rest for a while.'

'I have the rest . . . of my life . . . to rest. Stay.'

'Are you sure?'

'Show me . . . another trick.'

XIV

Andrews crosses the threshold, out of the hospital grounds and into the city, his city. This is the best time to see it. Darkness hides its brokenness, the gaps in its teeth, the cavities. At night, it becomes a majestic city again. Now, at Kristin-tide, it is better still, because what remains of it – the streets and squares that survived the rockets and shells – is lit up with strings of white bulbs and coloured candles burn in all the shop windows.

He wishes – not for the first time – that he were a stranger in his own city. He wishes he could walk the streets and not be seen, not recognised. But everyone who has worked at the hospital knows him, and that is just the beginning. It is a large city, but his circle of acquaintances is large too.

He walks into Eight Bells Street, slowly, and bathes in the glory of the shop windows. This is the street shown in international magazines to illustrate the city's recovery. This is the street where wool and cashmere suits are made to measure, where glass as fine as eggshell is shaped into champagne flutes, where imported designer jewellery is sold for more than a man could earn in a year. And in each window, along with the strings of Kristin lights, the saint is commemorated by displays of the traditional 'Light of the Eye'

icons, painted on to wood or ceramic bases, countless ornate painted eyes like peacock tails looking out
from the shop fronts.

On impulse, Andrews steps into a men's boutique
and walks to a rack full of sunglasses. Most pairs look
foreign and expensive, but he does not even glance
at the price tags. He tries several pairs on, standing
looking blankly into the long, thin mirror. As he
tries on the third pair, unable to discern any real
difference between them, he catches sight of his
grandfather pausing outside the shop, looking at the
glittering clothes, shoes and watches, and shaking his
head before turning up the collar on his rough tweed
coat and walking on.

'I think the heavier frames look particularly good
on you, sir.'

Andrews doesn't reply, but takes off the pair he is
trying on and hands them to the shop assistant.

'I'll take these.'

The assistant – young and immaculately dressed –
looks as if he could be parachuted in each morning
from another country, another world, a peaceful,
prosperous place where men have time to apply
moisturiser and condition their hair. Andrews swal-
lows hard as he hears the price of the sunglasses, but
he hands over a card, and asks for them to be left
out of their case.

'I'm going to wear them.'

The assistant smiles, assuming that Andrews is joking,
but the smile fades when he sees his customer disappear behind the thick black frames and lenses and
leave the shop. Is he famous or infamous? Who would

wear shades at night? The assistant stares after him, wondering if he's missed a celebrity encounter.

Andrews' eyes take a while to adjust to the darkness. His mind is already there, but his eyes feel old and slow. He leans against a mailbox while his eyes slowly open: full, vulnerable. After a minute, the streetlight is enough, and he walks on slowly, feeling more secure, more hidden. Is this what Jamie is doing now? Is Jamie adjusting his eyes to a new, much darker, or much brighter place? Is he ambling down a new but familiar street in a new and beautiful city? The thought makes Andrews want to cry again, but he bites his lip and holds back. That is enough crying. Enough tears. Now he can understand – as he didn't at the time – why he was so set against them taking Jamie's corneas for transplant. Who would want to send their son into the next world blind? It all makes sense, until he thinks of Jamie struggling for breath on that beautiful street in that beautiful city. He may still have his eyes, but what about his lungs, heart, kidneys? Would he need them? Has he sent his son into the next world unable to breath, to love, to speak, to sing? He thinks of Jamie witnessing everything for eternity, living in a world full of voices and poetry and songs, but because he has no lungs he has no breath, and because breath is the root of voice, he is rendered mute until the end of time.

'Trust in the Lord!'

The voice of his dead father stops Andrews in his tracks. It was not a still, small voice in his head, but a booming voice from the other side of the road. He whips off his sunglasses and scans the pavement opposite. He sees the back of his father, in his Sunday suit, disappear inside a candle shop, but when he crosses the road and peers in, the shop is empty.

A drink is what he needs. A man needs a drink at a time like this. What is the use of being a dry drunk anyway? You get all the grief and paranoia but without the hours of lightness and the nights of oblivion. He sees up ahead – on the corner of Eight Bells Street – the Spirit Cellars. Its proprietor, dressed like an old waiter in black tie and apron, stands in the doorway waiting for customers. The way he looks, he has been waiting for a long time. The spirit in question is *Ysu* – an icy clear drink with a tail of fire. The method of its making has been passed down through a handful of families in the northern mountains for centuries. It is rumoured to contain something of mountain stream and heather, something of bilberry and fox, but they are just rumours. It tastes of cinnamon and wood smoke, and it burns so bright that you can almost see it going down the throat and into the belly of a drinker across the room.

'You like to come in, sir? Taste some of the finest *Ysu* you ever tasted?'

Andrews shakes his head. He loves the bite of *Ysu*, but it's not just a drink anymore. When he first met his wife, he was working in a small town in the mountains, helping to run a maternity unit. He was fresh from university, and the midwives all took pleasure in mocking his Southern accent. All except Alicia. He was welcomed into her family and they married within a year. For her father, no evening was complete without *Ysu*, no guest was entertained without its fire. Even when the war broke out years later, Andrews would keep a bottle in his office and a bottle by his bed, but then the pictures came out in the papers. Northern warlords toasting a massacre with glasses of *Ysu*. Sales of the drink south of the border collapsed overnight. Only last year, the Spirit Cellars opened and was welcomed as part of the process of reconciliation. But it cannot shake off its associations.

'First one on the house, sir?'

'I can't. Really. I'm sorry.'

'War is over, you know. It's just a drink.'

The proprietor looks desperate and bitter. Andrews hides behind his dark glasses, shrugs and walks on.

'You a big rock star? You wanna sing a song?'

Andrews slows down for a moment, not in anger at being mocked, but with a sense of outrage. He wants to tell the man that his son died tonight, and that his wife – his Northern wife – is also dead. He wants to tell him that he's a recovering alcoholic, and that *Ysu* was his worst and best poison. But he quickens his step and turns the corner.

there is a need for ongoing training and appraisal to ensure that we move forward together, nationally and regionally

Bits of his work in progress, his hospital mission statement, keep floating into his head. He has been writing it for weeks, poring over every word, convinced of the importance of the exercise, but now the language seems so hollow.

As he enters the Market Square, he is missing Alicia

as well as Jamie. A wife killed in war, a son in peace, one by a random rocket, one by a mad dog. What difference does it make how they go? They go, and that is all. Perhaps they are together tonight. Maybe he wishes he was with them. He crosses himself and heads towards the huge bronze statue of St Kristin in the middle of the square. When Jamie was a boy he loved to see Kristin at this time of year, with her arms outstretched to welcome the world, and her eyes – even through the verdigris – fixed on the streets, the people of this city, her beloved people. Jamie loved to see the shivering mass of candles and nightlights and lanterns around the base of the statue.

Andrews stands with his back to the statue and surveys this, once the grandest plaza in the city. Now it looks like a gap-toothed crone. The art gallery restored with foreign money stands next to a music school collapsed into itself. The newly rebuilt American Embassy is two doors away from the former Opera House, a low priority for restoration and expensive too. He turns to face the statue, St Kristin almost alive in the play of the lights on her robes. He picks up a nightlight from a large box left for pilgrims, posts a coin into a slot in the statue's base, and places the light by her left foot. He steps back and the flame spits. He walks out across the square and when he looks back his flame has disappeared into one great light from hundreds of candles around Kristin's feet. For the first time he sees the statue as an execution scene, a woman being burned at the stake, holding up her arms to plead for rescue.

A Civil War in Nine Cigarettes:

5

The furtive one smoked by a man who shouldn't be smoking. As soon as he lit it, he felt a rush. He didn't even have to breathe it in. It was something to do with spending all his professional life cutting open chests and digging out diseased lungs, or stitching new lungs in. Something about the professional implications of a lung transplant surgeon being seen sucking on a filterless imported cigarette.

It reminded him of his youth, at the start of the war, when he and his fellow students would go into the most violent, sectarian bars in the city, dressed, of course, in full Southern patriotic regalia. They knew all the right songs, insults, gallows jokes, but they would wear a Northern paramilitary shirt under their own, or carry a Northern cap badge in a trouser pocket. It was the buzz, the adrenalin, the bluff, the sure knowledge that if anyone saw that badge or shirt the whole bar would be on top of you, tearing you to pieces.

So he stood in a coat and hood on a piece of waste ground in his home town. It was not just any piece of waste ground. He remembered it from childhood when it was the Tropical House. He used to love coming here. Now, nobody came here except vagrant war veterans and men with something to hide.

He had just come back from a trip to the North. It was the first time he had crossed that border since the war. He had brought something back with him, a treat for the feral dog packs in his city. He took another drag on the cigarette and coughed. He was not used to it. His cough made him drop the plastic bag he was carrying, and out of it a lung slid onto the rain-soaked rubble by his feet.

He panicked, glanced around. No one was there. No one was watching. He looked up, and there were no security cameras. He felt guilty. He felt ashamed. But not too ashamed. This was a filthy lung, a damaged lung, an old man's lung. He nudged the piece of meat away from him with his foot then he backed away. He took a long drag on the cigarette and watched. As he had hoped, stray dogs crept out of the shadows and started sniffing at the lung. One picked it up and trotted away towards the light. Suddenly, a man came into view, crossing into the wasteland through a huge stone archway. The surgeon threw down the cigarette and pulled his hood closer over his face. Maybe it was one of the government's dog killers. Maybe he would shoot the dog, then find the lung. That could be a disaster. Then the dog started growling. Good. The man was backing away. The dog was closing in on him, but what if the man saw the lung? What if — by some chance — he could see what it was? The surgeon gave a single shrill whistle, and watched the dog slink back towards him. The other man continued to back away. Nine times out of ten the whistle worked with these dogs. Feral, not wild. They still had a memory of discipline.

XV

She is crossing the lakes she used to visit as a child. She has flown over this region once before, in the afternoon when the sun was high, and the shadow of her plane surfed the lakes and forests below, towing her along like a child with a kite. Tonight is different. There is no shadow plane to pull her along. But she is not on her own. She has a boxed voice in the passenger seat beside her.

She keeps telling herself that the boy is dead, that his voice in her head is just her voice, her mind exploring another of its dialects. There is no boy in the box beside her, just a piece of human tissue. In fact, he – it – will be stitched into someone else's chest, wired up to their throat, their mouth, drawing breath so someone else can live, walk, talk. She feels sick.

A voice on the radio asks her how she is getting on. Air traffic control are not normally so solicitous. But she doesn't like being patronised. It is hard enough to make your way as a woman pilot without being treated like a learner driver, to be checked on and worried about. She tells them all is well, and signs off.

Take me down and show me the lake

The boy has stopped singing, and is asking her questions. She glances across, but all she sees is a cool box.

Show me the lake

Jude hesitates, keeps a level path. But the voice keeps pleading with her. Is it too much to ask? She wants to look at the lake too, because it's part of her childhood and it is so beautiful.

She pushes the plane down and banks towards the largest of the lakes. The trees give way to log cabins at the edge of the water. She remembers seeing them as a girl, and wondering if her family would ever get to stay in one. They seemed at the time impossibly opulent and luxurious. Her family would spend their holidays at a farm campsite down the lake road, but these families lived a different kind of life. She would watch them getting out of their big dark cars and carrying large suitcases into their cabins. The girls would wear dresses more expensive and beautiful than any in her mother's wardrobe, let alone her own. The fathers – businessmen or civil servants pallid from the city – would stand on the balconies in their too-bright shirts, smoking and gazing out across the lake.

Now the cabins are unlit, and even from above she can see that some are smashed into wigwams or bonfires.

Take me right down to the water

So she takes the plane lower to the borders of land and water, takes it down so low that she might wet its belly. Any lower and the plane will catch a crab, tilt, somersault and sink, but she is in control. Absolute. She can do this. And the boy beside her is singing now, singing an old song about the sea, about a boy king crossing the sea.

Speed bonny boat, like a bird on the wing, over the sea to Skye

He has a lovely voice – quiet but rich, like a choirboy, echoing inside her head.

'Could you confirm your position again?'

The voice on the radio cuts across the boy's song, stops him singing. She hears him muttering, whispering as she lifts the plane away from the lake and back on course. She gives out her position without emotion or explanation. She wants air traffic control to leave her alone until she needs to land.

Take me back to the water

But she doesn't. Now is the time to re-focus. She lifts and steadies the plane, climbing slowly until all below is black. Now they could be flying through the outer universe, the deepest ocean, the mind of a giant, the bloodstream of an even bigger giant. The lung next to her hears what she is thinking and starts a new song about a boy who slays a giant.

XVI

Now Andrews needs a drink more than ever, and he knows where he should go to get it. He heads down a narrow street off the corner of the square and past a row of boarded up shops. A group of teenage girls is hanging around in a shop doorway, dressed for a night out. They are laughing at him, he is sure of that, but he doesn't look across at them. A middle-aged man in dark glasses at night. He feels both invisible and highly conspicuous at the same time. Did these girls know Jamie? If they did, then why are they laughing, why are they out for a night on the town? Surely they should be grieving like he is, if they really knew Jamie.

Andrews crosses the road, almost getting run down by a taxi which flashes its lights and blasts its horn. This makes the girls behind him laugh even more. He wishes he could be their age, wishes he could be the one laughing. These are the fruits of the armistice: freedom for the young to stand on street corners at night and make jokes about the old. Fair enough.

He sees the lights of the Sports Bar blazing ahead of him, all the more dazzling in contrast with the sober old tobacconist's next door. As he passes the tobacconist's window, he turns his face away towards the street. Tonight, the death of Jamie has unleashed all the family ghosts and he wants them laid back to rest. The last thing he needs now is to see his father or his grandfather or one of the great-greats standing stoking a clay pipe in the shop window, slowly shaking his heavy head. However comforting they may seem at first, however consoling their words, he does not want to see them any more. He does not understand why he is seeing them. He dives in through the swing doors of the Sports Bar and breathes a sigh of relief.

Around him on every side is light and noise. It is bright enough for him to leave his shades on. In fact, he's not the only man in the bar wearing shades. It is one huge room, but with a large chrome and mirrored bar in the middle. There are large screens in every corner, showing different sports from different cable channels. In one corner, a group of young men is watching an ice hockey game. The game looks dull to Andrews, a cross between figure skating and golf with occasional punch-ups. But the spectators are shouting and cheering. They look like they have been drinking for a while.

Andrews goes to the bar and orders a double bourbon. He wants an *Ysu*, but he wouldn't dare ask for *Ysu* in a place like this. Sitting at the bar drinking that mountain brew is a fast track to a lynching even now. Catch a bunch of lads whose team has lost tonight and the guy sipping *Ysu* is just what they are looking for.

there is a need for ongoing training and appraisal to ensure that we move forward together, nationally and regionally . . .

A double bourbon is smacked down on the bar. Andrews helps himself to ice. Lots of it. Then he swishes it around to get the whiskey good and cold. He hugs it like a hummingbird between his hands, and feels its wings buzzing, its tiny heart shivering. He lifts it up and smells the rich dark sweetness of it, then swills it round the glass some more. He lifts it to his mouth and lets the faintest touch burn his upper lip and tongue. Five years. Five years of keeping off the stuff. Five years of keeping the promise he made to his wife. But surely, if there was ever a night to break a fast, then this is it. He lifts the glass again, but holds back just short of his lips.

'Here's to my boy. Here's to Jamie.'

He does not mutter his toast, he sings it out, and raises his glass as he does so. But the bar is pumping out so many commentaries on so many games that no one hears him. No one except the barman, who looks round and gives a smile and nod in response. Andrews knocks back half the glass in his first swig. He wants it to hit home fast. It tastes like strong cold caramel, but it does nothing. It isn't even as good as he had remembered. Whatever he had hoped for in his first drink after five years, this was not it. He drains the glass and waits to catch the barman's eye to get the same again.

A hummingbird again, something buzzing in his pocket. He puts his hand in and takes out his mobile.

'Geoff? It's Karla. Where are you?'

'In a bar. What d'you want?'

'Oh, Geoff. You're not . . .'

'Have you called to lecture me? Because if so . . .'

'No. No. This is important. The police found drugs in Jamie's things.'

'What drugs?'

'Cocaine.'

'Oh, well. He went to parties.'

'I have to ask you some more questions about his lifestyle.'

'Bit late for that, isn't it?'

'Can you come back to the hospital?'

'No, I can't.'

'I have to ask you . . .'

'Well, ask me now.'

'It's because of the lung, Geoff. They need to know if he used intravenous drugs. It's about HIV. I'm sorry. I have to go through this.'

'Of course he didn't.'

'They can do a quick screen, but there isn't time to run the full tests.'

'He wasn't a junkie.'

'Because of the cocaine, they were worried about the fuller picture.'

'There is no fuller picture.'

'Where are you, Geoff?'

'In a bar.'

'Can I join you?'

'If you must. But no more questions.'

'Which bar?'

'The one Jamie worked in.'

'Sports?'

'That's the one.'

He puts the phone back in his jacket pocket. He catches the barman's eye and holds up his empty glass.

Behind him another corner of the bar erupts into cheers. He turns to see on the large screen a footballer he doesn't recognise skidding on his knees towards the corner flag, arms outstretched in celebration. All his team mates pile on top of him, and in that corner of the bar men the same age as the player are hugging each other and shouting with joy. The barman fills up his glass, and Andrews takes a long, deep swig. Yes. Oh, yes. It's all coming back now. He is beginning to remember why he was a drinker.

XVII

Until the surgeon comes back it is going so well. It had never crossed the minister's mind that the carnival tricks she picked up from her parents would play a role in pastoral care. With kids perhaps, but never with old men. It is simple card stuff, the kind you can see on any city street corner in summer. Pick a card, any card. Don't show me, don't tell me. I want you to think about the card, picture it in your head but say nothing to me. It is the nine of spades, queen of diamonds, two of clubs, whatever. Foolproof. Right every time. She could do it all day with her eyes shut. After the disappointing chess game, Baras asks her for another trick, but something more relaxing than watching her juggle. She always keeps a pack of cards in her bag, so it makes sense. To her amazement, he is mesmerised. He keeps asking her to do it again and again. He rings the bell by his bed to summon a nurse and orders a new pack of cards, which is brought to him, and still she gets it right each time. It is a good distraction, but then Ross the surgeon comes back.

'Mr Baras, I need to talk to you.'

Ross pauses and glances at the minister, who stands up and starts on her farewells to the patient. Baras shakes his head.

'She can stay.'

The minister looks at Ross, who shrugs and carries on. The minister sits down again.

'Look, Mr Baras, the donor lung. I can't say very much about it, but there is a possibility of drug use on the part of the donor. I believe some illegal substances were found with the body. There is no evidence of intravenous drug use at this stage, but clearly it raises concerns about the donor's lifestyle and the possible risk of infections such as HIV and hepatitis.'

Baras looks wide-eyed, struggling for breath. He has said too much to the minister and now he feels that his breath is running out. He wants to ask questions of the surgeon, questions about the donor and the lung, but he can't summon the words. Ross sees him struggle, and speaks again.

'Your case is urgent, and suitable donors are rare. I think you should consider this carefully, but on the balance of risk, on the knowledge available to us, I recommend that you go ahead. I'm told by the doctors at the other end that it looks a good healthy lung. Obviously, I can't guarantee that it is free of infection, but at your age and in your condition I would think very carefully before turning down this opportunity. Without a transplant, there are great risks too. Pick up a cold this winter and that could well be it.'

The minister sees Baras' wide eyes, and can feel the fear coming back to him. He is unable to catch his breath well enough to ask a question, so she asks one for him.

'Can't you run more tests?'

Ross looks at the minister and sniffs, then he looks back at Baras to give his answer.

'Not before the operation. The cold ischemic time for a lung is less than six hours. By the time we get the results, the lung will be beyond use. And besides, HIV can be latent in the body for weeks before showing up on tests.'

Baras feels his breath returning, not as a gale, but as the lightest of breezes. Still, it is just enough to ask a question.

'What should I do?'

'The next of kin is being questioned about the donor's drug use and sexual history. If that raises further concerns you will be informed. But you do have to make a decision.'

Ross looks at them both, nods briefly and leaves the room. Baras closes his eyes and tries to settle his breath into a slower, deeper rhythm. Ever since his lungs were damaged, he has found it hard to see it as a failure of his own body. Somehow, even now on the brink of having his weakest lung cut out and replaced with a new one, he can't locate the problem in his own chest. Sure his chest is heaving as his lungs try to drag in the air, but it still feels like a problem with the air, not with his body. On that April morning so many years ago, the air itself was altered, and his sensitive lungs failed to adapt. His lungs are a genetic throwback to a time when mountain air was richer, warmer, more plentiful. His lungs were designed to take the cream off the top of the thick air, and now the cream has gone he cannot recalibrate. Everyone around him has adapted. Perhaps in the old days – when the air was strong – all these young people would have struggled with their rough, greedy lungs. They would have died of excess breath.

Baras feels the minister reaching for his hand and clutching it again between hers. But he doesn't want comfort any more. He wants something stronger, more conclusive.

XVIII

The boy sings another old song about a boy king. The voice sounds calm and that is good. If the voice sounds calm it helps her. The song is one she knows from years back, but she's never heard it sung as beautifully as this.

> *His face and hands were lily-white,*
> *His lips had never tasted night,*
> *His voice was yet to break with fear,*
> *His eyes were salt and diamond clear*

She sings along with him to give herself courage. Suddenly, the plane feels much smaller. The panel of dials and hands and numbers glows in front of her and now it means nothing. She breathes deeply and concentrates. If she looks at the dials one by one she knows exactly what they do, how to use them. Altimeter, Artificial Horizon, Ball Spirit Level, Turn and Bank. Yes, she knows all of them. This must be a familiar syndrome for pilots in early career, she thinks. On a long solo flight at night it's all too easy to have moments of panic. Steady the ship. Steady. That's better. That's right. The sky is benign and the plane won't let her down. Everything will be all right. It will be.

Jude has always been a fatalist, but a cautious fatalist.

It helps her to get through the day, knowing that somehow the world looks after those who look after themselves. Her husband Tom – as an arrogant young student – had tried to impress her with his counter-arguments, his courage, his commitment to living on the edge. Once, when they were sitting in his room late at night, they had heard the sirens crank up all around the city. He persuaded her to stay in his top-floor room, not to run to the safety of the shelter.

'Look,' he'd said. 'We live by chance. We're here by chance, and we'll die by chance too, unless we take our own lives.'

She had protested that by staying in his room they may be doing just that. It was suicidal.

'Chances are we'll be fine,' he said, 'and we'll be stronger for having risked it.'

He was right. They were fine, but the tower block next door to them was felled like an old tree and shook their building to its roots. At the moment it fell, she glanced across and his eyes were full of fear, full of what she was feeling. But when the rockets had stopped and the danger had passed, he was full of himself again, shouting and waving his arms about.

'Life is random, and everybody lies about it! Tonight we are fully alive. We'll be stronger now, you'll see.'

She felt sick. And sick of him. She had tried to leave, but he grabbed her by the sleeve. He had more to say.

'When a mother tells her baby, *There, there, it'll all be all right,* is she lying? Of course she's lying. She hasn't a clue what will happen tomorrow. Should mothers be lying to their children?'

She had wrenched her sleeve out of his hand and slammed the door behind her, furious that his games had put her life at risk, certain that the relationship was over.

The radio cuts in. Air traffic control want to know if she has hit bad weather yet. She says it's fine. They are calling to warn her that she might meet a squall further north. They will keep in touch if they get more detail. Just keep an eye out for it. That's what they tell her. Keep an eye out.

Jude tells them that all is fine, that the plane is in safe hands and still on schedule. She sits up straighter in her seat, tightens her grip on the controls. The lung is silent in its cool box on the seat next to hers. For a second, she feels like laughing at the ludicrous image of a picnic cool box as a co-pilot, sitting uselessly in front of its controls. But then she thinks of the boy again, of Jimmy, of the boy who gave his lung.

She takes the plane lower, hoping to discover some contours, to reconnect with the landscape. If there's a storm ahead, she wants to know where she is, to take some bearings from solid ground. Slowly the dark land rises up to look at her. She sees gentle tree-lined slopes, the fells that signal the start of border country. Here for centuries the old line in the dirt that marks out North and South has been smudged and redrawn. To the distant left she sees the lit stone face of a castle, one of a necklace of fortresses built by the North to keep Southerners out. The old Northern kingdom was at its height when it dreamt up these great castles, but their empire was pushed back over the mountains a century later. Now Southerners treat these castles as their own pride and heritage. In the civil war they became a potent symbol of Southern resilience, despite being built by the North. Well built, too, you'd have to say. They withstood all the rockets and the missiles thrown across the border, though some said Northern warlords couldn't bring themselves to smash up their ancestors' handiwork.

Jude hasn't seen a castle since she was a girl. She can't stop looking at it, sizing up its sheer face washed in honey coloured light. Why is it lit up? Even in this new peace the tourist trade is non-existent, especially this far north. No one comes to border country save the odd foreign journalist looking for mass graves. She banks away from the castle, as if to turn her head away. The voice of the lung is silent. The world seems silent. She feels very far away from home and destination. Flying over no-man's-land, she feels she has to break the shattering silence so she starts to sing. But the only song she can think of is the song that the voice in her head was singing before, an old folk song about a boy king:

> *His face and hands were lily-white,*
> *His lips had never tasted night,*
> *His voice was yet to break with fear,*
> *His eyes were salt and diamond clear,*
> *Yet when the gold crown kissed his head,*
> *A man was born, a boy was . . .*

When she reaches the last word of the chorus, she chokes on it.

XIX

Karla looks at his glass and shakes her head as she sits down next to him at the bar. He shrugs, asks her what she wants to drink. She orders a glass of red wine and the barman pours it in front of her. Andrews finishes his whiskey and orders another. She doesn't try to stop him, just puts her hand on top of his and says his name.

'Look, I'm a grown up. I can make choices.' He glances at her, gently takes his hand from under hers.

'So what's this about cocaine?'

'They found some on him. The police. It raises questions. Official questions. Because of the transplant.'

'Like I said, he wasn't a junkie.'

Karla takes a swig of her wine.

'How well did you know your son, Geoff?'

'What kind of a question is that?'

He doesn't meet her eyes. He pretends to be absorbed in the football match on the big screen. The players are crowding round the referee, pushing and spitting at each other, yelling at the referee. The referee is standing in the middle of the baying pack with his hands held up like a saint in an icon, trying to calm the waters.

'Geoff, I'm not saying anything about Jamie. I'm telling you the police found this stuff, and because of the transplant I have to ask questions about high-risk behaviour. I'm asking because I have to.'

'Well, he rode a bike. That was pretty high risk, as it turned out . . .'

'You know what I mean. High risk for HIV and . . .'

'I'll say it again. He was not a junkie.'

'So, not a high-risk lifestyle then?'

He turns to look at her, pauses, and fixes her with a stare.

'Nothing.'

Andrews turns back to face the big screen, shakes his head and drains his glass in one gulp. The serene referee looks less serene now. He is holding up a red card at one of the shouting players, who is being dragged away by his team mates. Then he turns round and shows the card to another player, then another. Each player recoils as though he's been struck with the card, not just shown it. Each player is dragged away from the pack and begins to walk off the pitch, spitting and cursing as he goes.

'You're saying Jamie's lifestyle wasn't high risk for HIV?'

'Oh, for God's sake, Karla. I'm saying that. Okay? Now shut up about it.'

'Okay.'

'You knew him too.'

She nods and looks down at her glass.

'Yes, I suppose I did.'

He gives the barman some coins and slides his glass towards him. On the big screen the referee is pointing at one of the remaining players, threatening him with the red card too. But the player is fuming, almost foaming at the mouth. The barman delivers a new drink, just as the player on the screen lets fly a punch at the referee. The man in black hits the floor, out cold on his back. Another player pitches in and head-butts the man who decked the referee. Now it's a free-for-all, one big punch-up. Match officials run in from the sidelines and the crowd begins to spill over the barriers onto the pitch. Andrews nudges Karla and points to the screen, but she's not watching. She is quietly sipping her wine and looking down at the polished wood of the bar.

'Sometimes I hate my job.'

'Join the club. Another drink?'

'Why not?'

'D'you fancy a game of pool?'

'What?'

Andrews mimes the action of pool player.

'I know what it is, but do you really want to play now?'

'What do you want me to do, Karla? Sit here and stare at the wall whilst I contemplate my grief?'

'Well, if you put it like that . . .'

'They've got some tables upstairs. Let's get another drink and go play. Jamie loved pool. And I'd rather do that than sit here and talk about his drug habits.'

'I'm sorry.'

'I know.'

Andrews gets two more drinks from the barman, gives him a note and asks him for change for the tables. As they head for the stairs, the scene on the big screen is one of chaos. There are now police with batons hammering members of the crowd. Every now and then one of the footballers emerges from the mob and makes a run for the tunnel. Men are swinging from the crossbars of a goal, which, as it snaps, is broken up and used to make weapons. In the left foreground of the picture, a man is on the ground being kicked by two other men. In the bar, a crowd is gathering to watch the spectacle, but this crowd is different, not baying for blood, but watching, wide-eyed, fascinated. Andrews and Karla stop for a moment and Andrews gazes at the screen. Karla watches him and looks across the faces of the others, lit by the huge screen in front of them. They are not so still and quiet because they're shocked, she thinks, but because this satisfies some need in them. Some of the faces are almost in rapture. She takes Andrews by the arm and gently leads him off towards the stairs.

At the top of the stairs, a smaller crowd has gathered in front of a smaller screen watching the same punch-up. Smoke bombs and flares from the crowd and tear gas from the police are making this scene look even more like a battlefield. Horses and swords would not look out of place. Men loom into shot and stagger across the screen with bloodied faces.

It is a large, open room with twelve pool tables laid out in a grid pattern. All except one are being used, so Andrews goes to the spare table, puts a coin in the slot and stacks up the rest of his coins on the side. He hands Karla a cue and starts arranging the balls in a triangle.

'I'm pretty good at this game, Geoff. You'd better watch out.'

Karla lines up a practice shot with an imaginary cue ball.

'We'll see.'

The drink is kicking in now. He feels light-headed and even light-spirited. If alcohol is a depressant, why does it feel so good? He remembers why he got hooked in the first place. It is a daily medicine for the ills of life.

A couple of minutes into their game, Andrews looks up at the screen to see two football fans lunge forwards and attack the cameraman. The picture tilts to one side, then seems to burrow into the turf before shutting down. The programme cuts to a studio where a panel of bewildered looking football pundits is waiting to dissect what is happening. The crowds watching the screen in the bar begin to drift away. Within minutes the screens are switched to another sports channel where a baseball game is being played, then they switch again to a music channel. As the music pumps out, a small entourage comes up the stairs, led by a photographer who stops the party and separates out one man. The man is tall, well-built, athletic. Andrews recognises him, but he can't put a name to the face.

'Who's that?'

Karla shakes her head.

Now the athletic-looking man is smiling and giving the thumbs up to the photographer as he poses with two young waitresses from the bar, then with an older man who looks like the owner or manager. Players on the other pool tables are stopping to look at him. Some are muttering to each other.

'Oh, God!'

Karla suddenly slams her cue down on the table and fumbles in her bag to find her phone.

'What was I thinking of?'

Andrews plays a shot, then looks up.

'What's the problem?'

'I forgot to call them.'

'Who?'

'About the lung. To say the lung's okay. Low risk. I'll tell them that?'

She looks at him, as if expecting some deeper reassurance.

'Tell them what you want.'

She takes her phone and heads off for the toilets, trying to find a quiet place to ring through the final verdict on the lung. Andrews settles to play another shot, then remembers it's not his turn. He sits on the corner of the table and watches the photographer at work. One last flash of the camera and the manager points at him, straight at Andrews. Some words are exchanged among the entourage, then the manager leads them over.

'Have you finished on the table, sir?'

'No. She's just gone to make a call.'

'Would you mind switching tables? This one's the most discreet.'

'We're in the middle of a game.'

The athlete whispers something in the ear of a dark-suited man standing next to him. The dark-suited one has a shaven head and looks like a bodyguard.

'Oi, mate!'

A young man on the neighbouring table prods Andrews with the end of his cue.

'If he wants your table, give it to him.'

Andrews stands up and points at the young man with his cue.

'I'm in the middle of a game. Why don't you just get on with yours?'

The young man curls a lip and leans in towards Andrews.

'He's a national hero. Who the fuck are you?'

Andrews glances at the manager to see if he will rein in this aggressive young customer, but the manager is nodding in agreement.

'Sports hero and war hero.'

The aggressive young man repeats the manager's phrase and holds his cue above his head like a javelin, as if aiming it at Andrews.

'Athlete and soldier. A hero.'

Andrews slams his cue down on the table and picks up his stack of coins from the side of the table. He knows he should keep his mouth shut, but he can't.

'What the fuck does that mean?'

The aggressive young man puffs out his chest. Andrews sees on his T-shirt the familiar symbol of a clenched fist and the slogan SOUTH AND PROUD. The young man's face is red and pinched.

'What?'

'I said what the fuck does hero mean? Haven't we learnt anything?'

At that moment, Andrews can see that he's one touch, one tilt, one word away from conflagration. How easy it would be to say something else, or to pick up his cue and swing it. Within seconds this place would look like that stadium on the big screen.

Somewhere inside him a voice says 'Why not?' He stands still for a second that feels like a minute, then picks up his coins, his coat, Karla's coat, and walks away through the middle of the entourage, which parts to let him through.

XX

On the nap of the earth, clinging to the globe's full curve, this is the way to fly. The wind is strengthening, but it feels less threatening down here as she skims above the treetops. Jimmy, the poor boy whose lung is in the box, the blind co-pilot, is silent. His voice is not in her head any more. But Jude sings and speaks instead to break the silence.

Suddenly the dark horizon rears up into mountains. This is the true border, although no one is supposed to talk about a border now. She lifts the plane and crosses the earthworks, mounds and trenches, the brick-built lookout towers and half-smashed walls. She flies low over strips of forest blackened and burnt to stubble. Every so often she glimpses the naked white flesh of huge broken trees caught in the moonlight. Mighty spruce and fir, majestic beasts once bought by towns across Europe to grace their civic squares, now only good for bonfires. Nap of the earth, under the gales, she sees a cleft between two mountains and heads for it. This is tough flying, this is flying by wits not by numbers.

The mountains must have taken the bite out of the wind. It is quiet and easy to fly. What were the air traffic controllers warning about? The squalls must have blown themselves out. The cleft below the plane becomes a valley, dotted with farms marked by pinpoints of light on the valley's ribs. At the head of the valley a mountain rises and she identifies it as the first of the Bleaks, a string of mountains that runs in towards the airport. She knows she should climb its gentle face and soar across the Bleaks to get her precious cargo to its destination as quickly as she can. But the gales might be stronger up there, so as she glimpses a narrow valley opening up to her right, she banks hard and enters it.

Much tighter and darker than the previous valley, there are no pinpoint farm lights on the sides, no road snaking through its middle picked out by a set of car headlights. As she flies further in, she sees a cluster of lights ahead. Their glare is powerful, and as she gets closer, she can make out the shapes of buildings. A large farm, a quarry or cement works perhaps. Maybe this is what is meant by factory farming, as rows of long plain huts come into view. Then, as she takes the plane lower, she sees the full scale of the place, its endless rows of long low buildings, exercise yards, watchtowers on the perimeter. She keeps flying down the valley and it keeps unfolding beneath her. There were always rumours that the North had huge prison camps, labour camps, death camps. But nothing was ever proven, nothing was said after the armistice. No one was held to account. A searchlight swings up and flashes across the plane. As it does so she cowers, waiting for the sound of gunfire, but it doesn't come. She lifts the plane out of the valley, and back on course over the Bleaks. As the lights of the compound fade, they give onto great mounds of earth, barely grassed. What kind of farming is this? Like massive ancient long barrows, like fresh graves for giants. Surely not, she thinks. Surely not.

Maybe her husband was right after all. Maybe the peace was a sell-out to the Northern butchers. How many people died in that valley? Her people. All those foreign journalists looking for the evidence of war crimes and here she is flying over it. Here she is flying one of her people – the lung of a terrified, silent boy – across the border to be handed over to a stranger, to be stitched into the chest of a Northern stranger. Can that be right?

'Yes, yes, I'm fine.'

She tries to sound calm when the man on the radio asks her if she is still on schedule. He has a strong Northern accent. Does he know about her detour? Does he know about what she has seen in that valley? If he does, then he is saying nothing.

'Any bad weather yet?'

'No, all calm. Thank you.'

'Well, keep an eye out.'

She is tempted to turn the radio off, but the voice is necessary now. It is the voice of her destination, and only that voice can clear her to land. Despite their name, the Bleaks are beautiful. No lights up here, but the snow makes it shine, reflecting the moonlight. In the distance, she can see the glow of the town. Why is the lung so silent? What has happened to its voice in her head? Is something wrong? Did they pack it properly in ice? Has it breathed its last in transit? Is it dead?

She reaches across and fingers the zip on the cool

box. She needs to check if the lung is okay. She opens the zip about an inch to feel its breath on her fingers. Nothing. What's wrong? The lid is held down by two plastic clips, but the zip keeps the cold in, seals it tight. She slides the zip open a couple more inches, and now she can feel the cold against her fingers through the gap.

The curiosity is overwhelming. Curiosity and concern, yes. But mainly curiosity. As the old pilot said, a quick glimpse can do no damage, since the thing is packed with ice. Suddenly, she knows she has to do it. She reaches across with one hand and fumbles with the plastic clips. She flicks up first one clip, then the other. She takes a deep breath. Steadies herself. Her fingers feel for the zip again. She slowly pulls it past one corner and across the front. Then leaning right over she manages to pull the zip open on its third side.

'We're expecting you in about fifteen minutes. Okay?'

'That sounds fine.'

This time, she does turn the radio off. No more interruptions. She is the custodian of this lung. She is responsible for its welfare. She needs to check on it. A quick look will do no harm at all. Without glancing at the cool box, she feels for the lid, now hanging loose above the box, and pushes it fully open. A rush of cold air hits her face. But silence too. There is no voice in her head except the echo of her own. She is utterly alone.

A Civil War in Nine Cigarettes:

6

The one lit to mask the smell of linseed as a blackwood flute was oiled by hand. This was like coaxing a frozen, wounded creature back to life. He worked the oil deep into the wood with his fingers, especially into the cracks. He wanted to heal it. He was an old man now, without the breath to play it well any more. It could sit in its box and crack on a shelf, or it could be kept alive and passed on, like a story, to the next generation.

His wife was in the next room, stitching, mending. What was the difference between mending a shirt and healing a flute? He knew she would not approve. She didn't mind him smoking, but the linseed smell would have her in here asking questions. She always hated the sound of the liquor-stick. Even though it should be in her blood. She was born in the mountains, and that stick is the voice of the mountains.

He finished the oiling, closed the box, wrapped it in brown paper and addressed it. What would his wife think if she could see this? He could hear her in the next room humming as she stitched. She was humming the same tunes he would play on the flute if he could still play. The same tunes, so what difference would it make?

He was not sending this to his grandson to make trouble. He would put a card in with it, warning the boy to be careful where he played it. Surely with this new and fragile peace such things could be allowed again. If a grandfather could not send his grandson a family heirloom then the peace was not worth keeping. These traditions mattered. This flute had to be cherished, even in a Southern city. The boy may have been raised as a Southerner, but this was a piece of him too. Roots.

XXI

'Forgive . . . an old man?'

'Forgive him for what?'

Baras takes the minister's hand and lays it on his head, uttering on her behalf the words he wants to hear.

'I absolve . . . and deliver you . . .'

She takes her hand back and smiles at him.

'You know, I've never met an atheist with such a craving for the sacrament of reconciliation. One could easily mistake you for a man of faith.'

He asks for her help in sitting up higher, and he focuses on her again. She asks him if he wants a cup of tea or coffee. He says no, but she gets up and fetches a bottle of water from the table in the middle of the room. She takes his empty teacup and half fills it with water, then she puts it on the table by his side.

She makes small talk about the room, about the weather, about the Lucy-tide lights and decorations in the streets outside. He listens and breathes deeply and slowly, taking in as much air as he can. Then he reaches out and puts a finger over her lips like a parent shushing a child. She recoils, looks away, folds her arms in front of her.

'Sorry,' he says, 'I didn't mean . . .'

She nods to reassure him, but her arms remain

folded, and she doesn't catch his eye. He draws a deep breath and tells her a story. It comes out in fragments, broken by long breaths and pauses while he gathers strength. She keeps wanting him to stop, but she can see the effort he is putting into the telling, and she knows it must be important to him. Know when to be quiet and listen. It's there in all the training. Know when to sit back and let them talk.

His story goes back decades, to his university days. As a postgraduate, he and his friends had been allowed into the anechoic chamber. Built up with cement, fibre-glass, rubber, this room within a room within a room was like being inside your head. Out of curiosity he asked to be locked in it alone, but after ten minutes he was screaming to get out. No one could hear him. When they did let him out after fifteen minutes he was suicidal. Why? Because it was like an inner hell. When the door shut behind him, he had spent a minute marvelling at the deadness trapped between those honey-comb walls, singing to test it. Then the silence had sucked him in, and he had stood in the middle, listening to the most complete absence he had ever known. After five minutes, he was lying on the floor listening to his own heartbeat, the tiny squeaks and groans of his lungs, the brush and slide of his eyelids every time he blinked. Five minutes later he was up at the door, hammering and screaming, having glimpsed the chasm inside himself.

The minister is looking at him now, but her arms are still crossed. The story has taken a good ten minutes to tell, and has used up so much of his remaining breath. She can't see why it was worth all that. But he hasn't finished.

'Do you think . . . Pascale . . .'

She nods. It's important to look attentive.

'. . . that the chasm . . . was my soul?'

He rests and draws another breath. She opens her mouth to say something, but he hasn't finished.

'. . . or was it . . . the place where . . . my soul should be?'

He looks at her as if he's expecting an answer.

'I have no idea, Mr Baras.'

She fishes around in her bag, looking for her Bible. It is an old translation she always carries on the hospital rounds. The older patients are comforted by the language, even if they don't always listen to the words. She wonders if reading him a passage might calm him down, might even keep him quiet for a while.

'I have been . . . afraid of silence . . . ever since.'

He stares at her, still in hope of some response, but she flicks through the Bible – clearly at a loss – and begins to read from the Psalms.

'I will say of the Lord, He is my refuge and my fortress: my God; in him will I trust. Surely he shall deliver thee from the snare of the fowler, and from the noisome pestilence. He shall cover thee with his feathers, and under his wings shalt thou trust: his truth shall be thy shield and buckler. Thou shalt not be afraid for the terror by night; nor for the arrow that flieth by day.'

She is expecting Baras' eyes to close, hoping that he may drift off to sleep so she can leave. But he doesn't. He leans forward and slowly swings his legs down from the bed, then he sits on the edge of the bed and pushes himself up. She puts the Bible down, and stands up to help support him.

'Is this wise, Mr Baras? You're supposed to be resting.'

'The window.'

He points across the room and she slowly leads him there. He rests on her arm as they look out across the dark rooftops and the streetlights. On the horizon, two planes are circling with their lights flashing, queuing up to land. She is expecting him to say something about his city, or his people, or his life. But he can't or doesn't want to. All he does is lean towards the window and breathe on it, then he wipes the mist away with the side of his hand.

XXII

Andrews stands outside the corridor to the toilets, waiting for Karla. He can see her hunched at the end of the hallway, covering one ear with a hand to focus on the phone call, engaged in earnest conversation. She has her back to him. After a few minutes waiting, he goes back to the barstool where his evening here began. The barman obviously hasn't heard what happened upstairs, or he wouldn't serve him. Who would serve the man who snubbed a war hero?

The phone behind the bar is ringing. The barman wipes his hands on a towel and answers it. The call is short. He beckons to a waitress to mind the till and pumps, and he hurries off. The waitress glances across at Andrews and smiles at him. He smiles back, perhaps for too long, because she busies herself drying glasses at the other end of the counter.

'Excuse me!'

The waitress comes over and reaches out to take his glass.

'Another?'

'Yes, but just before you do that, I want to ask you something.'

She glances behind her, perhaps wishing that the barman would come back and rescue her. Andrews realises that he's slurring his words. What must she think of him? What question is she expecting?

'Look. My son used to work here. James Andrews. Jamie. I just wondered if you knew him at all.'

She shakes her head.

'Name doesn't mean anything. Sorry.'

'Are you new here?'

'Fairly. How long ago did he work here?'

'Okay. Never mind.'

'Perhaps another sports bar? There's one by the university.'

'Yes, perhaps.'

'Is he looking for work here? They're after another barman.'

'No. No, he's not thanks.'

Andrews looks away towards the corridor where Karla is, but there's no sign of her coming back. The waitress takes his glass and asks him what he'd like. She blinks when he orders, not sure she's heard him right, but he repeats it and hands her a large note. A couple of minutes later his glass comes back full of whiskey – six or seven shots – and she sets down a bottle of still water next to it. Andrews drinks some of the water, then tips the rest into half-full beer glass on the bar. He slowly tips the whiskey into the empty water bottle, screws the top on and pockets it. A takeaway.

He looks around, the big screens have switched from music to baseball. Why don't they just show war footage? Archive from the bloodiest battles and sieges? That's what people want. Especially with a war hero playing pool upstairs. Why fill the screens with pseudo-warfare when you can watch the real thing? They should make a film of his finest moments in the athletics stadium intercut with his finest moments on the battlefield.

The Way Forward – Strategies for Integration and Cooperation in Modern Healthcare.
Section Three: The Challenge of Sectarianism.
Through effective management, staff can take ownership of their own future, as stakeholders in an integrated healthcare system. Far from an attempt to deny our recent history . . .

The words of his own mission statement whisper in his head like a prayer, an incantation. But they mean nothing. They might as well be random sounds assembled to aid meditation, stripped of all associations, flayed of meaning, blank. Andrews turns his collar up and looks back at the corridor where Karla still stands welded to her phone. He looks at his watch. Surely she will finish soon. She has to finish before that manager or one of those pool players comes back downstairs and finds him still here. He stares at the bottles behind the bar and whispers under his breath.

'Far from an attempt to deny our recent history . . .'

'Why aren't you up at the table? We hadn't finished playing.'

Karla sits down next to him.

'I'll explain later. Shall we get out of here?'

He drains the last drops from his glass and stands up ready to leave.

'I should go home, Geoff.'

'Why?'

'I just should.'

He takes her arm and leads her towards the door. They step outside and the night air meets them with its cold hands.

XXIII

As soon as the lid is open she is reassured. There is ice there. She can feel it. The medics made a decent job of packing up the lung. She scans the instrument panel in front of her. All is well. She is enjoying flying with the radio off. When it's on, even when there is no voice, there is a constant white noise in the background, and now the only sound comes from the twin engines of the plane.

'How silently, how silently, the wondrous gift was given . . .'

For a moment Jude thinks the lung is singing again, but she looks across to the passenger seat and she can't hear it anymore.

She thinks again of the old pilot who had given in to temptation and opened a transplant box. He had told her what he'd seen inside. From that glimpse he concluded that human hearts were not always scarlet or crimson, some at least were marbled purple and yellow like a bruised fist. He said it changed the way he saw people after that. Knowing they had these bruised fists inside them. It had never crossed Jude's mind to want to see what a liver or kidney or heart would look like. Anyone who has been to a butcher's shop has seen it all before. Meat is meat. And yet . . .

Although they say the heart is the seat of emotion,

and the liver is the seat of life itself, there's something different about lungs. You don't see lungs on butchers' slabs. Why not? Are they inedible? No. She remembers her grandfather feeding his dogs with the lungs of pigs and sheep. He said the breath in them would give the dogs more vigour, extra stamina. He used to call this lung food 'lights' and since he lived so long and kept so fit Jude always suspected that he ate a share of 'lights' himself.

What is their secret? Is it in the breath as Granddad said? The breath of life held in the lung even after the rest of the body has died? Or is it spirit? Same root, same place. If you eat the lungs of an animal you eat its soul.

The sky ahead is clear now and the ride smooth. Jude switches on the autopilot and turns towards her co-pilot, her passenger, her charge. Reflected snow-light from the mountain tops fills the cockpit. The unzipped, unclipped cool box is now fully open to the air. Just a quick look, to check if the lung is okay. It's part of her duty of care. A quick look, that's all.

Gently, her fingers push aside the crushed ice from the top of the box to reveal a clear thick plastic bag. She finds the top and pulls the bag open with both hands. Cold air and the smell of the preservation fluid. There it is. This is Jimmy's lung. This is Jimmy's soul. She had imagined it as white, bleached or colourless, but it's grey, an ash grey. The top of it is cone-shaped and looks like a sponge. She shifts the bag and peers further in. She can make out alveoli like little grapes on a vine.

She leans across for a closer look, then she hears a

sound like breath being drawn, not slowly and deeply, but a short, sharp breath like the breath between sobs. Perhaps it was the crushed ice shifting, or the plastic bag rustling, but it sounded like a sob. Crying is the first sound we make, the first breath we take when the midwife slaps us on the back. Perhaps it is the last sound too, laid down like a seam of coal so deep within the lung that all our words and songs and wishes have to come out first before the crying comes. Is this crying simply the final breath of a lung?

She sits up, staring through the window at the Bleaks ahead and below. She checks on the automatic pilot then lowers her face towards the bag again. Silence. Nothing. Perhaps it was the bag settling. She can't touch it. She might damage it or give it germs. But her hand reaches in anyway, and before she knows it she is feeling its chill, almost too cold to touch, soaked with preservative and tears, but more fibrous and tougher than she had imagined, as hardy as a rare polar lichen. She pulls her hand away quickly. No harm done. The very lightest of touches. She pinches the top of the bag together and brushes the crushed ice back over the top.

Sometimes the weather changes slowly on a flight, then at other times it hits you like a wall. This is one of the other times. One moment Jude is leaning over the cool box as the plane flies through the so still darkness. The next moment she is trying to keep the plane in the air when the storm wants to rip it from her hands.

In daylight these gales would be terrifying. At night, hours from home and flying over mountains, it's hard to imagine how she can keep the plane in the air. She cries for help, she prays, but no voice comes to answer her, to calm her down. She can see nothing beyond her own cockpit, just a magenta darkness through the streams of water on the glass. Having felt so solid on the ground, the plane now feels as light and fragile as balsa.

The gales fight each other for control of the plane. She stares as the instruments judder and settle and judder again. This is what they mean when they talk about 'flying by instruments'. In training, it all seems so simple: lock your eyes on the dials and keep the needles steady, make smooth corrections, forget everything outside the cockpit. Suddenly, this business of flying seems brutish and physical. It takes all her strength and all her wits to keep it going. She cries for help again. Again silence. The instruments should be comforting with their gentle backlights, but now they are a series of random needles and numbers. She could be in the deepest ocean or outer space. She is lost.

XXIV

'What the hell d'you think you're doing?'

Ross waves the minister out of the way and takes Baras' hand, leading him back to the bed.

'This man is less than an hour away from the biggest operation of his life. He should be resting.'

The minister helps Baras by taking his other hand. Escorted by both of them, he settles again on the bed.

'I'm sorry, Professor Ross. He wanted to look out of the window one last . . . well . . . before the operation.'

Ross appears not to hear the minister's explanation. He stands over his patient with a look of cool concern, gently placing a hand on the old man's chest as he watches it rise and fall. There is an electronic alarm and Ross takes a pager out of his jacket pocket. He looks at it intently for a few seconds, then switches it off and puts it back in his pocket.

'I need to know what you have decided. The lung will be arriving soon and we have to start making preparations if you want to go ahead.'

Baras nods slowly, but says nothing. He does not make eye contact with the surgeon. Ross stares at him.

'Are you saying yes?'

Baras shuts his eyes.

'A nod is not enough, Mr Baras. I need to hear you speak it.'

He stares again at Baras, who does not open his eyes or his mouth. A tiny fruit fly loops around his face, a refugee from the cold outdoors, a rare breach in the hospital's hygiene policy. The minister watches it riding Baras' weak, slow breaths. She tries to wave it away with a hand. Ross is locked on to Baras.

'Well? Mr Baras?'

The minister stands up, smacks the fruit fly between her hands and wipes her hands on her cassock. Baras opens his eyes suddenly, to see the minister and Ross standing face to face over him. Her eyes are blazing.

'What are you playing at? He nodded, didn't he? He's here, isn't he? He's been here for hours. What do you need? Written permission?'

Ross is unflinching.

'Preferably, yes. But in this case I'm prepared to accept informed verbal consent.'

'Well, he nodded. So leave him alone.'

'Look, madam. You may deal in speculation, I have to deal in certainties. This is a life threatening operation, and the law says I need full patient consent to . . .'

'Yes! Yes! Yes! For God's sake, yes!'

Baras shouts his consent, with more breath behind his voice than either of them thought he possessed. Ross nods, says a curt thank you and tells the minister that she must leave when his team arrives. Then he leaves.

'He doesn't like me.'

She grins at Baras. But Baras isn't smiling. He is

drawing deep from the oxygen mask. He looks anxious now and she thinks his eyes are getting moist. Please. This is what she dreads. This is what the seminary tries to prepare you for, and fails to. If a man old enough to be your grandfather breaks down in tears of remorse and terror before a major operation, what do you say? What do you do? Where do you find the authority? The gravitas? Pray for it. Pray for it and it will come. Pray for it and it may come.

XXV

'Will you stop drinking if I make you a coffee?'

'It's my house. If anyone makes coffee it's me.'

Andrews is rooting in his pocket for his house keys. He takes a fistful of change and stares at it, swaying slightly as he tries to see straight. The house is in a dimly-lit mews and it looks elegant, newly painted white. Its owner does not look elegant, with his suit half shed and a fistful of cash spilling on the floor. Karla tries to help him sift through it, but it's all money, no keys. He takes another dig in his pocket, opens his hand again and leans against the front door for support. The door gives way as his shoulder meets it, and he falls through onto the hall floor.

'My God, I'm always telling him to lock . . .'

Andrews' words fail him, and Karla helps him sit up. He looks stunned.

'This is going to happen, Geoff. There will be times when you'll say things as if Jamie were still here. It's all right to do that.'

'Don't counsel me, Karla.'

He struggles to his feet and shuts the front door behind him. Karla switches on the hall light and follows Andrews into the kitchen. It is several years since she has been in this house, but everything is as she remembered. The kitchen is immaculate, a little out of date but the granite, wood and chrome are clean and uncluttered. The cooker still looks unused, although she knows he is a fine cook. She offers to help him, but he makes the coffee himself, stage-by-stage, starting with the chilled beans from the freezer where he always kept them. She asks the odd question, to break the silence, but she can see he doesn't want it broken. He doesn't mind if she just sits and watches him, so that's what she does.

'A little milk?'

He holds up the bottle.

'Not any more. Have to watch my weight.'

'You don't. You look fine.'

He stares at her a little too long and she looks away.

'Do you still cook, Geoff? You used to like it.'

'Are you hungry?'

'No. No. Just asking.'

He doesn't answer, but hands her a coffee, splashing it on her fingers as he does so. She yelps and puts her fingers in her mouth, but he seems not to notice. She follows him into the living room. As ever, it looks like a show home. Full and empty. It has all the right things in it – coffee table books of exotic cities, bowls of pebbles and pot pourri, a piano in the corner. But it has no stamp, no sign of life, no personality. When she was with him, she would try to change things, leaving earrings on the arm of a chair, or her shoes under the piano. But she found he couldn't live with it. He tidied them and gave them back to her. Now, he's taking a bottle from his pocket, and she realises why he didn't make himself a coffee.

'Whiskey?'

He holds up the bottle from the sports bar – his takeaway – to offer her a shot.

'No. And I thought you were drinking coffee.'

'Why would I do that?'

He takes a swig from the bottle and sits at the piano. She has been dreading this. He lifts a small thin case from the top of the piano and opens its latch. He takes out a silver flute piece by piece and starts to assemble it. He purses and puffs through his lips as if he's about to lift a weight, then lifts the silver flute to his mouth and blows across it. A strangled, broken note. He takes the flute away with one hand, lifts his glass with the other and takes some whiskey. It burns, and he exhales hard as if he can breathe fire. Then he takes up his flute again and blows a clearer note, then two, then three. She watches his lip curl as he makes an exaggerated embouchure, then relaxes into something like the real shape. The more he plays the clearer the notes come, until he's halfway through what used to be his signature, his audition piece. Perhaps this time, she thinks, the balance is right. Perhaps for once he's drunk enough to relax him, to overcome his block, to get his lip to make the embouchure, but not so much that his fingers fall away. He plays a duff note, takes the flute away and has another drink. Now his eyes are closed and he is playing Vivaldi as Vivaldi intended. This – she thinks – would honour any concert hall. But then it starts to falter. A finger slips off a stop. The top lip tightens and a note becomes a screech. He keeps playing, then drinking, then playing, but it's gone. In one movement, he takes his right hand off the flute and throws it aside with his left. It hits a bookcase and clatters down onto the floorboards.

'You had it there, Geoff. For a minute you had it!'

She gets up and collects the flute, running her fingers down it to check for damage. She takes it to the piano, gently pulling its sections apart and putting it back in its case.

'You mustn't give up. You had the lip then, I could see it. I could hear it. You got the lip back and you played.'

Andrews is looking at her. Staring. But he isn't listening to her. She reaches across and strokes his hair.

'Is it broken?'

'No, it's all fine.'

'Pity. I should have smashed it years ago.'

'Don't be like that.'

She keeps stroking his hair and, to her surprise, he lets her.

'I don't know what I'm grieving for, the son I knew or the one I didn't. When we were expecting Jamie I was sure it was a girl. We had names for her, and clothes and everything. When he came out, it was the best moment of my life, but there was a tiny death too. When my son arrived my daughter vanished. What if that keeps happening? What if they turn out to be someone else?'

'I don't know what you mean.'

'No one at the sports bar knew him. What was he doing?'

'No one? Who did you ask?'

'A waitress.'

'One waitress?'

'Yes. One.'

'Well, then.'

'What did he do, Karla? Did he talk to you? If he wasn't in the bar what was he doing?'

'It's not important now.'

'It is to me. Was he dealing drugs?'

'A little. And he wrote codes, viruses, spyware.'

'Why?'

'Money? Fun? He was young, Geoff.'

'Why did he tell you these things, and not me?'

She shrugs.

'Because he didn't have a mother to tell? Because I was around a lot?'

'But *I* was around a lot. Always.'

'You're his Dad. There are things . . . well . . .'

For a moment, Andrews looks desperate, as if he's going to break down again. She puts a finger to his lips, and then she kisses them.

XXVI

Found. Not just found but rescued. The storm clears as suddenly as it came. Now the sky is taking shape beyond the glass in front of her. Not an endless deep darkness, but a sense of scale again, perspective. Now she sees a star, a constellation. Jude laughs, on her own in the plane, out of sheer relief. There is a rush to it, to keeping the crate in the air against all odds. A storm like that in the mountains at night would challenge a pilot with ten times her flying hours, but she gritted her teeth and she did it. She met it head on and prevailed.

The radio has been switched to silent for ten minutes or more. She turns it back on and waits for air traffic control to speak.

'We lost you there. About to put you down as an emergency. What's going on?'

'Don't worry. Bad weather. Radio playing up a bit. Got it working now.'

The airport is within a few minutes' flight. Jude tries to gather her wits again. She checks all the instruments, re-establishes herself as the one in control; professional pilot on a mercy mission.

The outskirts of a town are beginning to take shape below. It looks very different from her home city in the South. Even in the glare of streetlights, she can see that the colour of the stone is darker, cut straight from the mountains. But the spread of grey stone is far from unbroken. Just as at home, there are gaps between buildings, but the gaps are wider and the piles of ruins much higher than in her city. So, the North was hit hard too. So it should be. This is justice. She is flying over proof that there is justice in the world.

As she approaches the airport the gaps widen between buildings. Now they are chasms, not gaps. She flies over mile after mile of rubble. Was is it more than justice? Overkill or underkill? More or less? She can't decide whether to be pleased or sorry about the wreckage below her. There are no cranes or building sites. Reconstruction here has barely started. The airport lights are coming into distant view and air traffic control is talking her down.

As she starts her descent, the pattern of grey stone and ruin breaks into a blaze of smaller lights and colours. At first she thinks it is a festival or pilgrimage, but then she sees the shape and scale of it. A shanty town. A shanty city. Row after crooked row of shelters in wood, plastic, corrugated metal. She thinks of the children living there. She doesn't know what to feel. It looks beautiful from the sky, this makeshift metropolis. It looks all the more human for its irregular grid and scattered colours. It looks like a huge patchwork quilt, she thinks. But then she feels guilty for thinking it, because she knows it won't be keeping children warm tonight, on a cold damp night in the mountains. Poor children. Poor city.

She glances across to the passenger seat and sees the cool box standing open. O God O God O God what has she done? She hit the storm before she managed to close the cool box. The crushed ice at the top has a film of rust over it as the surface of the ice begins to melt into the preserving fluid. The plastic bag is slightly open, and the cone of grey lung inside is just visible. She has to get the box shut again, or she may drown the lung. With one hand and one eye on the plane, she reseals the lip of the plastic bag and flips the lid of the cool box down. She reaches across for the zip and pulls it round until it's shut. Then she fastens the clips. The box is sealed. The runway lights are clear ahead of her. She hums a lullaby under her breath.

A Civil War in Nine Cigarettes:

7

The one stubbed in an old man's face one morning in a prison camp. The old man had been there for many months since his village was attacked by border-raiding soldiers. Those who were not killed were taken prisoner.

This particular April morning he was shaving in the washroom when the guards came looking for him. The old man had – they said – been telling stories in the camp, and some of those stories had leaked out into the world beyond its walls.

The stories were about his village and what happened when soldiers from the other side came. One of his stories was about a young mother cradling her hungry, crying baby. It was about the soldiers who cut the baby's throat to make it quiet. Another story was about a grandfather like himself, forced to kill his own young grandson, then to cut out the boy's liver and eat it. It was about the grandfather dying hours later of sheer grief and horror. The old prisoner had more stories about what happened to the women, and what became of the men who tried to fight back with shotguns and farm tools.

The prison camp authorities didn't like the old man's stories. The stubbing of a cigarette between his eyes was only the start of what they did to stop him telling them.

XXVII

She is doing card tricks and he is crying. This is not going well. When Baras broke down she thought she would try to cheer him up, to distract him. He had liked the card trick so much that the minister felt it was worth another shot. He still seems to like it, and he still can't work out how she is doing it, but he is quietly crying and that isn't good.

She takes the cards and puts them back in the packet. Then she puts her hand on his and smiles. She doesn't know what to say. She wants him to stop crying but she can't find the words.

'I am ready.'

'That's good, Mr Baras. The medical team will be here soon.'

'No. I am . . . ready to make . . . my confession.'

'You told me already. About the past. The women.'

'There is more.'

She wishes she had stuck with the card tricks. Now she has a crying old man begging absolution from her. She wishes she was with another patient. Someone quiet and easily comforted.

'There was . . . a village . . .'

She waits while his breath allows him more words.

'. . . in the war . . .'

She lets his hand go, and places her own hands in

her lap. Whatever he is going to say, she doesn't want to be holding his hand when he says it.

'We were desperate . . . were ordered to use . . . chemicals . . .'

The minister gets up suddenly and walks towards the table, turning her back on him. Two fruit flies loop above the fruit bowl which has been left out too long. She puts her bag on the table and opens it, tipping it over at the same time. A packet of cigarettes falls out, and she hurriedly puts it back inside the bag.

'We were . . . ordered . . . to release gas . . .'

She turns back to look at him.

'So your lung . . . ?'

He nods.

'We were caught . . . when it blew . . . back . . .'

She is shaking now. She takes the cigarettes out of her bag again. She pulls one out and taps it on the table.

'If I go to the window, can I smoke? I know this place of all places. But I just . . .'

He nods, and gestures towards the window. She opens it and a cold draught enters the room. She peers out into the darkness, lights a cigarette and takes a deep drag, then she leans down to the opening in the window, and blows her smoke outside. She switches hands with the cigarette, and rests it on the window frame to try to keep the smoke out of the room. Her voice is faltering, and she feels like crying herself.

'I know all about that. Read about it. Massacre they called it.'

He shakes his head.

'No . . . choice.'

She smokes with quick, nervous movements.

'What do you want from me, Mr Baras?'

'Absolution.'

'I can't do that. I've told you. This is between you and your maker.'

'I am . . . self-made.'

'Well, you can absolve yourself then.'

She turns her back on him, facing the dark window, but she sees a clear reflection of him in the glass. He raises his hands towards her.

'Please . . .'

Without turning round she takes another drag and answers.

'What are you confessing? You say you had no choice.'

'A man can . . . refuse orders.'

She turns round to face him, and her cigarette smoke clouds into the room.

'You'd have been killed for disobeying orders, wouldn't you?'

'Maybe . . . I should have . . . refused.'

'Are you saying you're sorry for what you did?'

'I am . . . trying to say . . .'

She takes a final drag on the cigarette, then stubs it out on the window frame, throws it outside and shuts the window. She comes back and sits next to him. Her breath smells of tobacco and he feels a sudden craving for a habit he gave up on the day of the massacre, the day he lost his breath. Now, perhaps sharpened by the nicotine or the cold night air, perhaps inspired by the Holy Spirit, she finds she has some words. She has a role here after all.

'So this is a guilt you have carried for years. I can see why you want to be free of it, and I do want to help you. Have you talked to others about it?'

He shakes his head.

'It has been a burden on you, and now you have reached the point where you can say – in all honesty – that you regret what you have done, that you believe it was wrong, and that you want to be free of the burden. Conscience, Mr Baras. Conscience is a life changer. Our thoughts have an audience. That changes everything, doesn't it? Your thoughts have an audience. Isn't that right?'

Baras looks at her, but his mind is elsewhere.

'It was . . . terrible.'

'Yes, you have terrible memories. Now you want to lay those burdens at the foot of the cross. You want to walk away from them.'

'. . . terrible.'

'Are you genuinely sorry for what you have done?'

'I don't . . . know how . . . to repent.'

'It's not a word I use. Think of it as sorrow, regret. Are you genuinely sorry for what you have done?'

'Look at me . . .'

She sees a tired, stubborn old man, close to death, struggling for breath. She sees his tidy clothes, his neat, short hair. She sees his moist eyes and his small hands with their loose gloves of skin. She sees a man who wants forgiveness, but doesn't know how to ask for it, or to receive it.

'I am a . . . broken man . . .'

'I can see the damage the war has done to you. But if you want forgiveness, if you want reconciliation . . .'

'Absolution . . .'

'All right, if you want absolution then you have to turn your back on what you did.'

'Turn my back . . .'

'Yes.'

'I did.'

'You do?'

'Yes.'

XXVIII

Neither of them can sleep, but they both think the other is sleeping. Andrews stares at the glass of water by his bed. He took it upstairs with him last night, when he still had a son. He washed down his pills with it and left it half full. Now it has pinpoint bubbles floating in it, and flecks of dust on its surface. In the curved glass he can see the sweep of his room, lit by the standard lamp in the corner and the glow of the streetlights outside. He is shocked when he realises they didn't draw the curtains. But the people in the house across the road are never there. And besides, who cares? He does. He cares that he was stupid enough to do that. And now he wants another drink.

The empty litany of his unfinished mission statement murmurs in his head . . .

Through effective management, staff can take ownership of their own future, as stakeholders in an integrated healthcare system. Far from an attempt to deny our recent history . . .

No longer does it offer comfort, even as an abstract incantation. Now it is a song he can't get out of his head, a song he hates but can't stop humming.

Karla is lying with her back to him. She is gazing

through the window at the glow of lights. She is cold and she gently pulls the covers over her. She wants to go home. She wants him to be all right. She wants to stay. She wishes she had never left. She hears a siren and watches the blue flashing lights grow and pulse across the room before they fade to nothing.

Andrews slowly swings his legs out of the bed and sits up. Karla puts a hand on his back, but he shifts away. He gets up and draws the curtains, then he starts to get dressed.

'Geoff. No one need know.'

'D'you think I care about that?'

'It's all right, you know. We have a history. Sometimes those feelings come back and . . . well. It's okay.'

She gets out of bed and walks towards him wrapped in her bed-sheet robes. She stands in front of him and smiles. He pulls the covers off her and drapes them back on the bed, straightening them as he does so. Karla is left cold and naked in the centre of the room. He looks her up and down. She seems so familiar. Her body is full and firm. Her skin is olive toned, but still unmistakable in its near translucency. He sees her now, more than ever, as a creature from the mountains, a Northern woman. Above her breasts, a chain around her neck holds a locket. Whose picture is inside it? All the months they were together, she would never let him look. Perhaps it wasn't a picture at all. Maybe it was a lock of her mother's hair, a rare diamond.

'Have you finished?'

'Finished what?'

'The examination.'

She picks up her clothes and starts getting dressed.

Andrews straightens his trousers, finishes tucking in his shirt, tightens his belt.

'Is that part of the service these days? It's a long time since I've been on a counselling course.'

Karla stops in the middle of buttoning her blouse and stares at him.

'What did you say?'

'Sex with bereaved parents.'

'How dare you!'

Andrews looks away. His head drops. Karla quickly finishes buttoning. He speaks quietly without turning to face her.

'I'm sorry. I am . . .'

She puts her jacket on and roughly ties her silk scarf around her neck. She looks for a mirror, but there isn't one. She walks out and down the stairs, shutting the front door behind her. He follows, opens the door and steps outside. It is raining. Light rain just thicker than mist. Karla has gone. Lost among the traffic and drinkers and clubbers at the end of the mews. Karla is gone, but his mother is coming instead. Here she is, coming out of the busy street towards him, taking off her gloves. She looks unhappy. His father is behind her, trying to catch her up. Andrews pulls his front door shut and runs out of the mews past his parents. This time they don't even glance at him, and when he looks back they have vanished.

XXIX

Inch perfect, and in the rain too, on a wet runway. She tries to feel the glow as she has done in the past, the rush of satisfaction at bringing this beast out of the sky and planting it so gently on the runway that the passengers barely look up from their newspapers. The passenger. She has killed him. She knows it. She has drowned him by opening the box.

Jude rubs her hand on her jacket and the side of her seat to try to get rid of the smell, the stench of the preservation fluid. It isn't going. She thinks it will be on her hand forever. She has been told to taxi round to a hangar on the fringe of the airport where a car will meet her.

The boy is silent in the box. The boy is dead. She knows it. She taxis slowly past the smoked glass and steel terminal buildings. These are brand new. What is the point of a state of the art airport when the people are living in metal shacks just down the road? First impressions. Get the airport done, then foreign businessmen will want to come, then they will feel like spending money here.

She passes a plane from the South, like hers, but a passenger plane. Scheduled flights. That could be her in five years' time. At least it looked that way before she made such a mess of this job. The flying was fine though. The flying was fine, she reminds herself. And the lung might still be fine too. If the car comes quickly it could still be good enough. Passengers are climbing down the stairs from the scheduled flight and running the short distance to a shuttle bus to keep as dry as possible. She watches a couple with three young boys herding them across the concrete towards the bus. The boys look bleary-eyed and confused, looking up and blinking in the rain.

She taxis past all the planes into a dark corner of the airport where a single light shines above the door of a locked hangar. There are no car headlights, so she has got here first. She hopes and prays that the car will come soon. She positions the plane so she will see the car as it arrives. She switches off and the silence is heartbreaking. Somehow, she feels that the plane has been keeping the lung alive. It feels almost as if she has turned off his life-support machine. Her first instinct is to switch the engine on again, but she knows it's ridiculous. Come soon. Come now to pick up the lung. Come quickly or it will be too late. It is too late. She knows it.

To speed up the process when the car arrives, she takes the cool box by the handle and climbs out of the plane. It is noticeably colder here than at home. She shivers and puts the box down on a dry piece of the runway apron. In front of her is a puddle of rain-water with a shimmering rainbow on the surface. She leans down and washes her hand in it. She shakes off the drops then wipes her hand dry on the back of her jacket. She sniffs the hand, which smells vaguely of fuel and stone, but with the ghost of preservative fluid still present. She leans down and repeats the process. In the distance, twin lights are growing larger. She decides to say nothing about the lung. She thinks it is best to treat it as a box, as a delivery. She was asked to take this box from A to B and she has done so. She has nothing to say about the contents of the box. Not a word. She is simply doing her job.

The twin lights turn into a car, and it comes to a halt fifty yards in front of her. A terrible thought strikes her: what if this is the police, come to question her about her journey, about what she's seen. If the searchlight at the prison camp had glanced across her then it wouldn't be hard to track her down.

XXX

'O Lord, we bring before you Mr Baras, your child. You know what he has done, and you know that in his heart he has turned away from that.'

The minister leans forward in her chair by the bed. Her eyes are closed, and her hands rest palm up on her lap. Baras' eyes are open, fixed on her face.

'Mr Baras is truly sorry for his actions, and he asks now to be set free from the burden of guilt. Lord, breathe into this man your healing spirit, and be with him as he goes through his operation tonight.'

She opens her eyes and looks up, waiting to see if he has any words of his own to add. He does not.

'Amen.'

She pauses for a moment, as if saying her own prayer, or waiting for the answer to his. He shifts uneasily on his bed. She smiles and takes his hand again.

'There. I'm glad you were able to share that with me.'

Baras looks cold, empty. She looks into his eyes, no longer moist but dry and clear. He slowly shakes his head.

'I felt . . . nothing . . .'

'Nothing?'

'I wanted . . . absolution . . . not prayers . . .'

The minister picks up her bag and stands up. She feels she ought to have some response, something to say to this recalcitrant, selfish old man, this man who has made her feel useless and tied up all her time tonight. This country is full of people with burdens of guilt, that is the particular scar left by civil war: the constant reminders in the eyes of your friends, the stories, the buildings. Everyone has wronged a neighbour or a relative. What makes him so insistent on 'absolution', yet so arrogant in response to forgiveness? She thinks of all the genuine penitents, all the real needs waiting for attention in this city, and decides not to waste any more words on Baras.

There is a knock at the door and Professor Ross hurries in with two nurses. He stops in the middle of the room and sniffs the air.

'Has someone been smoking in here?'

The minister walks past him, towards the door, but she turns in the doorway.

'It's your patient. He couldn't resist one last drag.'

She heads down the corridor, but Baras points after her and Ross calls.

'If you've been smoking in here I'll have you banned from the hospital.'

The minister stops and comes back. She is furious. She stares at him and wonders for a second whether to hit him, or to hit Baras, or to light the whole packet of cigarettes and shove them in their mouths.

'Do you know, Professor Ross, you can tell a lot about someone from their attitude to smoking.'

'Don't talk nonsense.'

Ross opens the window to clear the air. He tries

to ignore her, looking out across the city and exaggeratedly breathing in the fresh air from outside. But she hasn't finished yet.

'Have you ever heard the phrase "He who seeks to save his life will lose it?" Think about it, Professor, when you have a moment. You could argue that non-smoking is a form of idolatry.'

'Get out of here.'

The minister smiles and leaves the room.

Ross fusses around the room and around Baras. He is gentle now, calming his patient with reassuring words about the lung being in good time and the team all ready to go. One of the nurses opens the door into the secret room, the en suite operating theatre. She flicks the lights on. From his bed, Baras can see the room shiver into fluorescent life. The other nurse leans over the bowl of fruit on the table and wafts her hand above it to chase away the tiny flies. She picks up and examines an apple, then takes the bowl out of the room.

A Civil War in Nine Cigarettes:

8

The one smoked after a fine meal of carefully selected imported food at a semi-derelict hotel straddling the border. No mountain hare, no silverside, no sweetmeats, no carafe of Ysu, no dishes that might carry the stamp of one side or the other. Instead, they ate food from the far east and the far west. Neutral food.

They sat around an oval table in a former ballroom, once bejewelled with great glass chandeliers. The shattered crystal had been swept away and the generals and warlords sat in near silence eating a meal as solemn as the last meal of a man about to hang.

Despite appearances, it was a first meal, not a last. This was the armistice table, and the new era of reconciliation began that evening in the kitchen. Two head chefs, one from each side, two commis chefs ditto, two waiters. Crucially, two lawyers, nervous of each other and the generals, shuffling the paperwork that came round with the coffee.

Deadlock broken with signatures. Accountable disarmament. Reopened borders. And a guarantee of no recrimination, no revenge, no prosecution of the leadership on either side. A clean slate. Hardliners on both sides had called for justice, but that would mean an endless cycle of revenge, of strike and counter-strike. The majority of people on both sides just longed for peace. Giving up on justice was a small sacrifice.

The lawyers stacked the papers, bowed in unison and left. The warriors sat in silence until one took off his tunic, rolled his sleeves up, lit a cigarette and raised a glass.

'Let the dead bury their own dead. Here's to the living.'

XXXI

Andrews arrives at the police station and straightens his jacket and shirt. There is no need to let these details go. It is late at night and he has lost his son, but if you let these habits go you let everything go. He likes to look smart. He tells the duty officer who he is. The duty officer goes to fetch a colleague. He explains what happened to Jamie, and says he's come to collect his son's belongings. There's a lot of discussion and paperwork, but finally they tell him that his son's belongings are no longer here. They were taken to the hospital with the body, once the drugs had been removed. It is the last place he wants to go back to, but Andrews returns to the hospital. He knows where Jamie's things will be. No one passed them on to him. He gets the master keys from security and unlocks Karla's office. As soon as he opens the door, he hears a sound across the room. He flicks the lights and sees Karla curled up on her office sofa covered with a blanket.

'Geoff? What are you doing?'

'I'm looking for Jamie's things. Working late?'

'I can't go home just now.'

'Why not?'

'Not good at home.'

'The new man?'

'Not so new.'

'So how long've you been sleeping in the office?'

'A few nights. I'll get a place. Just haven't had time.'

As she's talking, Karla gets up and unlocks her desk drawer. She takes out a tatty black drawstring bag and hands it to him.

'There's something in there – apart from the drugs – I didn't tell you about.'

'Never mind. I'll find it.'

He turns and heads down the corridor. She runs to the door and shouts.

'Where are you going now?'

'I don't know.'

'I'm worried about you.'

'Don't be.'

He leaves the hospital clutching a bag containing his son's last effects. What do you do with such a bag? It doesn't feel right to stand under a street light and go through it. It's a final connection with Jamie, and it must be afforded some dignity, solemnity even. He walks the streets, in search of a place, the right place to look inside the bag. Wherever that may be. On the corner of Eight Bells Street he sees the proprietor of the Spirit Cellars still standing outside his empty bar trying to coax these sullen Southerners into trying *Ysu*. The man recognises Andrews from earlier in the night, even without the shades, and nods to him.

'You change your mind, sir? Like to try some *Ysu*?'

'You're open late.'

'I'm always open, sir. Try a little?'

'Yes. I will.'

The proprietor looks astonished and delighted. He ushers Andrews down a steep wooden staircase and into a dark smoky cellar. It looks like the crypt of an ancient church, staked out with stone pillars, huge alcoves and candles. Andrews peers into the half-light and sees a couple sitting close together at a corner table. They peer back at him. It's a good place to meet someone you shouldn't be meeting. He leaves them to it and sits in the opposite corner at a large round table. He glances across the room and sees his mother in her winter overcoat kneeling and praying in front of a stone pillar. He blinks, looks again and she has gone. The proprietor comes and lights the candle in the middle, slides a round leather coaster in front of Andrews and gently places a clear glass full of even clearer liquid on it.

'On the house. First one.'

'Thank you.'

Andrews drinks and closes his eyes. It is everything he remembered. It is more than a drink. His lids are shut, but he feels them flickering like an old film projector. In the dark crypt of his head he sees a carnival of mythic beasts, a lightning show of everyone he's known, flash frames of each second of his life. This is hallucinogenic, mysterious, miraculous *Ysu*. And how he's missed it all these years.

He opens his eyes and picks up Jamie's black bag. He pulls the string and looks inside. It's too dark to see much. He reaches in and pulls out a small wooden box with a brass clip. He unclips it and lifts the lid. Almost immediately, he slams it shut and puts it back into the bag, then he slowly gathers his wits, takes it out and opens it again. In the box, a dark green cloth covers the four sections of an oiled blackwood flute.

The smell of linseed catches in his throat as soon as the lid is open. Silver bracelets hold the barrel sections together, but parts of the wood are cracked with age and overuse. The last time he saw a flute like this was at his father-in-law's house in the mountains more than twenty years ago. During the war, even the sight of a flute like this would have the owner locked up or lynched. This was a more powerful symbol of the North than any mountains or monuments. More potent even than *Ysu*. This is an incendiary instrument just lying in its box. But to play, well, that would take it to another level. As soon as it struck up with some lament or reel the sound would chill the heart of any Southerner. No matter what the song – about a long-lost lover or a lake at dusk – the voice of this liquorstick would be enough.

Andrews lifts one of the barrel sections out of its box. It feels cold and heavy in his hand. He runs it under his nose like an expensive cigar. Suddenly the proprietor is at his side with a bottle of *Ysu*.

'Now that is a beautiful thing.'

Andrews hurriedly wraps the flute back in its cloth and shuts the lid.

'All friends here, sir. Don't worry.'

Andrews doesn't know what to say. He knows he doesn't look like a Northerner, but sitting drinking *Ysu* with a flute like that, he can't be a regular Southerner either. The proprietor pours him another *Ysu* and waves aside the money Andrews offers.

'Where you from, sir?'

'Now, now. We're not supposed to ask those questions any more.'

'D'you play it?'

He nods at the flute in its box.

'No. I don't. Can't. My son does. Did.'

'Good man. It's important to keep these things going.'

Andrews nods, thanks him for the drink, and sips the *Ysu*. He stares down at the table in silence, until the proprietor has left him. So his son had some rebel fire in his soul? Andrews feels a rush of pride. Jamie must have been given his grandfather's flute, and carried it around perhaps as a talisman? As an act of defiance in this Southern city? Had he come down on the Northern side of his mixed ancestry? Andrews remembers many conversations about the war, and several about the death of his wife, Jamie's mother. His son was always passive on these occasions, sorrowful, reflective. Andrews concluded that – like many children of the war – Jamie wanted nothing to do with either side, nothing to do with the old wounds, the old lies. As a mixed-race boy, he had a major stake in peace.

Andrews drinks up and leaves a few coins on the table. He walks out with the bag across his shoulder. Now he knows where he is going. What he doesn't know is what he's going to do when he gets there.

No dogs. Not a single terrier sniffing in the alley. Not much traffic either. You wouldn't think that a boy was killed here just hours ago. A car thumps past with hi-fi cranked up and windows down. Across the road, the illicit couple from the corner of the Spirit Cellars walk home, parting in a doorway with a peck on the cheek. Andrews steps into the road. No sawdust, no twist of blood, no oil, nothing. It is as if it never happened. He glances across at the fence by the roadside, and sees a small collection of flowers tied to the railings with string. A woman is tying a single rose to the top of the fence. It is Karla. Andrews calls to her. She turns around and her face is wet. He thinks it's the rain, but when he gets closer her eyes are red and swollen.

'What's this about, Karla?'

'You.'

She looks down at her shoes, and at the rain pooling around them. Andrews tilts his head back and stares up at the sky, at the blankness. He tries to keep his eyes open, tries to stare into the heart of it, but the rain in his eyes keeps him blinking. He looks down again at the drenched woman on the pavement in front of him, head down, sobbing in the rain. He doesn't know whether to hate her or hold her. So he asks her.

'What do I do now?'

His voice cracks and he looks up at the sky again. Karla reaches for his hand, but as soon as he feels the touch he steps back into the road. A van screams past, swerving and blasting the horn as he falls into its path. It's one of the government dog-control vans. A dog barks from the wasteland between buildings across the road, as if it knows what's coming.

'Where are those fucking dogs?'

He turns and peers across the road, teeth clenched.

'It wasn't dogs, Geoff. Did you believe that?'

'The police said he was knocked off his bike by dogs.'

Karla shakes her head, slowly and deliberately.

'Strange dogs. I used to tell him not to busk. He'd stand outside the stations and play his flute. He said he was busking for money, but he knew what he was doing. Playing a flute like that with the way he looked. It was only a matter of time before someone reacted.'

Andrews looks baffled.

'The way he looked? What d'you mean?'

She laughs. She is pitying him now.

'Northern! He's a Northern boy . . . was.'

She looks down at her shoes again.

'Can't you see it? His mother's blood in him.'

'Are you saying he was murdered? By whom? War vets?'

'I'm not saying that. I don't know. But there's still plenty of people out there who don't think it's over. Why would he jump the lights? Was he being chased?'

Andrews shakes his head and runs his fingers through his wet hair, to push it back from his brow.

'No, Jamie had lived here for years. He was mixed race.'

'Did you ever see him cross himself?'

'He wasn't a churchgoer.'

'But he crossed himself from right shoulder to left. A Northern boy. He even did it at his mother's funeral when everyone else was doing it like so.'

She crosses herself from head to heart, from left shoulder to right, then back to the centre.

'Why?'

'Because he was angry. Because he believed these things mattered. Like I say, a Northern boy.'

'It'll never go away, will it?'

'What won't?'

'The hatred.'

Karla frowns and nods her head slowly.

'Yes, I think it will. It has to. I thought you believed that too, Geoff? There has to be a way forward, but it won't be quick, our history . . .'

She reaches out and touches his arm, half supporting him. He lifts his eyes and looks at her. She smiles at him, then speaks.

'If we give up on that? Well . . . I have hope. I do. I still do.'

Andrews pauses for a moment then reaches into the bag again and takes out the flute box, holding it in front of him. He wipes the top of the box with his hand as the rain gathers on it.

'*A way forward* . . .' he mutters.

Karla points at the flute.

'Be careful. That meant the world to him.'

He throws down the bag, tucking the flute box into his jacket pocket, and walks across the road without looking each way for cars. On the other side, he stands for a second, picks an alley between buildings and disappears down it.

XXXII

No checks, no clearances. A man in a dark suit gets out of the car and walks across to her. She is waiting for the usual official procedures – confirmation of identity, authentication of the contents – but none of that happens. He says something about the weather, and how he hopes it wasn't too rough a flight, then he leans across and takes the cool box from her.

For a second, she wonders if she will ever be able to let go. She feels a need for some greater ceremony, something to mark the passing. But she does let go, and he walks off with the lung, the boy, with Jimmy. At least it's not the police. No questions about the route she took. All she has to do now is turn round and get back in the plane, but she hears herself call after him.

'Excuse me.'

The man stops and turns round.

'I just wondered if you knew where it's going.'

He pauses for a moment, and she knows she is overstepping the mark. The good transplant pilot should not ask about the donor, nor the destination of the lung. The good transplant pilot takes a box from one airport to another and flies home again. End of story. She smiles, feigning general curiosity, trying to pass it off as small talk. He smiles back, and gives an answer.

'St Cedd's Hospital.'

'Do you know who's going to get the lung?'

As soon as she says it she regrets it. He looks mystified, then angry.

'Worried about it going to some filthy mountain man?'

'Of course not. I never . . .'

'You should know better than to ask.'

He looks her up and down with contempt, then turns and takes the cool box to the car. The car revs up more than it needs, and swings in front of her with its lights on full, causing her to shield her eyes. She watches the lights disappear into the distance. She sniffs her hand again and the smell is still there, the smell of the fluid, the smell of the lung. She kisses her fingers. She fishes for the mobile phone in her jacket pocket, switches it on and sees it hook up to a local network. She stares at the screen for a moment, waiting for the message icon to appear, but it doesn't. Sometimes it takes a while for the message alert to come through. She presses 1 and listens for her husband's voice, conciliatory, apologetic. But it isn't his voice. It's the recorded voice of a woman telling her that she has no new messages. She switches off the phone, takes a deep breath and climbs back into her plane.

XXXIII

Baras is flat out on the operating table in the gleaming chamber next door to his hospital room. He is wired up to various machines. They offered to explain all the machines to him, but he said he didn't want to know. He had lain there wondering if the donor lung was already present in the room.

He hoped, almost prayed, that his Southern donor lived a good life, that the lung was strong and healthy. He could feel himself blushing, sweating, hoping that the anaesthetic would come any moment and usher him away into a deep sleep.

He had an injection, to help him relax they said. At first it was a warm feeling, a feeling of letting go. Then it started to bite, and now it's agony. He can't breathe. His lungs won't move when he tells them to. The message is not getting through. He cannot move a lip or a finger, but he isn't feeling sleepy any more. He is screaming inside his head, but his body won't utter a sound. He can't move his head, but he can see the Professor and his team bustling around, wheeling trolleys of electronic instruments alongside the bed. Are they going to operate on him like this? Do they know he's still conscious? He is drowning, and he cannot move a muscle. He can feel his heart thumping in his head, but everything else is dead. To make things worse, a tiny fruit fly from the bowl next door has got into the room and keeps crossing in front of his face. No one else seems to notice it. What if it gets inside the wound when they operate? What if he's still awake, and sees it happen?

Ross leans over Baras, looks into his eyes. He lifts the eyelids wide and peers in. Baras wants to scream the roof off, but he lies as silent as a corpse. He tries to channel the scream through his eyes. If Ross sees the scream, he doesn't say so, just moves away to carry on preparing for the job.

All Baras wanted from this was to wake up with stitches in his chest and breath in his lungs and the whole thing over and done with. Now he is trapped inside his own corpse, desperate to animate it, to run and smash the window and drink in massive draughts of mountain air. His sight is going, his eyes are closing. He is drowning in a white room, an airless chamber. He is about to die before the operation has begun.

Pain. Like a knife in the throat. Then he is flooded. Ice cold air as thick as water fills him up. He feels inflated. He feels he can float. His sight comes back and there's a tube in his gullet. He is no longer drowning. They have given him air, but still nothing moves. He cannot even move his eyes. He just stares straight up from the bed. He wants to suck at the tube like a parched man at a bottle, but he cannot suck. He takes the air it gives him. It is just enough. He is still alive, but utterly helpless.

Ross leans over him again, about six inches from his face. After staring for what seems like minutes, he smiles.

'Mr Baras?'

Ross pauses for a moment, as if hoping for an answer.

'Let's call you by that name, although we do know it isn't your real name.'

Baras can feel his heartbeat racing, panic rising, but he cannot even flinch.

'We have given you a muscle relaxant, and some air. We can keep you in this stasis for as long as we want, as long as is necessary.'

Ross' lips break into a broad grin. But his eyes aren't smiling.

'Let me tell you about my surgical team, Mr Baras. We work together all the time. We have worked together throughout the war, and the things we saw, the terrible wounds we tried to heal, stay with us today. We cannot forget them. Those experiences bind us together as a team. We are the best transplant team in the country, and that is why the powers that be arranged for us to fly up from the South to operate on you tonight.'

Baras feels alone and desperate. He wishes he had insisted that the minister stay with him throughout the operation. Or one of his children. Or someone off the streets. Anyone from his city, his side.

'It is important, Mr Baras, that you listen to what I am going to say. This operation carries significant risks, and mine might be the last voice you ever hear. So hear this: You are helpless, you can't move a muscle now and we have complete power over you, the power of life and death. But you are in a comfortable hospital, and if you die on this table you will die with dignity and your past will be glossed over. That is the nature of this peace, clean slates all round. But let me tell you this . . .'

Ross leans in closer, so his lips are almost touching Baras' lips. For one bizarre second, Baras thinks he's going to kiss him, but Ross clenches his teeth and spits out words instead.

'Your slate will never be clean. You have the blood of my people on your slate. You had the power of life and death over thousands and you chose death for them. I have that power over you now. How does it feel? Eh? What did you tell the vicar about your sick lung? Did you tell her you smoked too much? Did you tell her you were the victim of a gas attack? Or did you tell her that you were the butcher, the bastard, that you were the one who gave the orders? Did you tell her?'

Ross is spitting, furious. One of his nurses puts a hand on his shoulder to try to calm him, to pull him away, but he shrugs her off.

'Let me tell you this. When I realised who you were I nearly went straight home. I nearly refused to do the operation. Then I saw it as an opportunity, a chance to meet you. A chance to meet the man who fed his prisoners to his dogs. Is that right? That's what they say. You kept a pack of dogs and starved them, then once a week you'd throw some sick or feeble prisoner in with them. Yes? And then you'd watch. Yes? My people. Not just prisoners. My people. And now, one of my people has offered up his lung to give you breath. That's us, you see. That's us in the South. Generous to a fault. Forgiving.'

Baras is longing to die now, longing to get this man out of his face, to get this tube out of his throat. If he could will himself to die, he would do so. He tries to will himself to die, to burst his own heart, but nothing will break it.

'I've read the reports. I know about the death camps. I know you grew so fond of those chemicals that you insisted on flying with your men when they dropped them, until that day when the gas bit you back. What were you, Number three? Number two? One even? Were you the king of the Northern warlords? I think so. I never believed that collegiate crap, there must have been one mind behind such evil. And I think it was yours. So let me tell you "Mr Baras", peace or no peace, I think you should be on trial for war crimes. I think everyone should know what you did. I think you should be up there on the TV screens as an international pariah. Or dead. Dead would be a good second best.'

Ross moves away suddenly and Baras hears a whispered argument between him and the anaesthetist. Then his face appears again in front of Baras.

'Are you a religious man, Mr Baras? I imagine not. But you never know. I've seen the pictures of your priests blessing the AK47s, sprinkling holy water on the rockets. Do you know what crucifixion is? Do you know what kills you? Do you think they bled to death? No. It's breathlessness. With nails through your hands and feet, your chest slumps and you cannot draw a breath. You have to push up on your feet to open your chest with every breath you take. And that is agony, of course. Eventually, you cannot push down on your feet any more, and you die of asphyxiation. Sometimes, the Roman soldiers would take pity and break the legs of a crucified man to hasten his death. But sometimes they would leave him to run out of breath in his own time. So I suggest you find it in yourself to pray. Pray for breath, Mr Baras. Pray now for the breath that you denied so many others.'

Then the anaesthetist injects something into the cannula in Baras' arm. Within half a minute the patient is unconscious, but just as he slips away, in the last seconds of his awareness, he thinks he sees Ross lean over him again, and spit into his face.

XXXIV

He can hear Karla's voice calling after him as he walks down the alley. Like so many parts of this city, the majestic row of buildings facing the street is little more than a façade. Pick any alleyway between the glass tower blocks and the sandstone tenements and you enter a wasteland. Bombs or rockets blew holes in the city, and no one can fill them in fast enough. The policy is to do the main street fronts first, the historic areas, then to deal with the gaps later. But no one has got around to dealing with the gaps.

Andrews picks across open spaces dotted with bonfires and makeshift shelters from the rain. In parts of the city there are small shanty towns – shanty villages, he thinks – set up by the bombed-out, the uninsured, the orphaned, the unlucky, the lost. Most of them are soldiers who never quite came back from the war, soldiers who can't live with peace. They gather under polythene and tarpaulin here, in one of Europe's great cities. One of Europe's formerly great cities.

He walks between rows of shelters, aware of the fact that he's wearing a business suit, but unconcerned. Some of the residents of this shanty village are dressed in paramilitary uniforms. Outside one shelter is a flag of the Southern axis. Another has the emblem of a fist. Andrews feels nausea rising from his belly.

He walks through a stone archway, all that's left of some once grand civic building held up by its keystone. On the other side, he finds himself among heaps of shattered glass, wood and iron.

The tropical house had been a favourite haunt of his before the war, and he wonders now what became of the lizards and the hummingbirds, the dinner-plate-sized butterflies and vivid snakes, the cloying heat. It isn't hard to climb the chain-link fence around the ruins. Others have clearly done this, because there's a rough path, a low track through the rubble. He walks in and follows the path into the darkness. The site is overshadowed by huge new office buildings on either side. Away from the streetlights it is very dark indeed. He can make out the odd light flashing off the broken glass, and the huge, brooding presence of the heap of rubble. Something moves on the path ahead of him and he stops in his tracks. He should never have come here. He tries to make out what it is. Too low for a man, too tall for a rat. The dog growls, arching its back. He wants to kick it in the teeth, to smash its skull and throw it on the heap of rubble. Is this the dog that ran into the road? Is this the dog that killed Jamie? It moves towards him slowly, snarling as it does so. It seems to be carrying something in its mouth. A piece of meat. He knows he should not run, and as the dog gets close enough to show some teeth he slowly backs away from it. Look away. He remembers his father saying you should never look a violent dog in the eyes. Look away. He backs slowly away, but out of the corner of his eye he sees the dog following him, inching closer. A short, faint whistle comes from somewhere further down the path, and the dog suddenly crumples, cowers and slinks back into the darkness. Andrews turns and heads for the street, but his path is blocked again. His grandmother stands on the path between him and the way out. She is looking at him with a patient smile, her eyes beckoning him to see what she holds in her cupped hands. As he approaches, he sees that her face is bathed in an iridescent glow, and in her hands, no bigger than a bumble bee, is a fabulous blue humming-bird. She opens her hands a little wider and the bird zips away past his head. His grandmother smiles, but Andrews walks straight through her and out towards the street, the living city into a square, small and dimly lit.

He has sometimes wandered through here in the daytime on his way to somewhere else. It is the oldest square in the city, formed around St Sulpice's: the oldest church. On a sunlit lunchtime, it's a colourful square, with its clutch of small bookshops and bars. The bars are all named after Southern saints, and the antiquarian bookshops are full of the works of great Southern poets, full of seditious nationalism in dusty hard covers. If Karla was right about Jamie's looks, he surely never came here at night. Now, when all the colour has gone, and the shop doorways are full of drinkers, it looks like a different place, a different era. The bars are in their night clothes: draped in flags and banners officially banned since the ceasefire, but here they know that a blind eye will be turned. People are staring at Andrews. His clothes are formal, but he is quintessentially a Southerner, and people here will have a nose for that. No one here would pick a fight with one of their own. Not unless he asked for it.

He walks into a crowded bar and loudly asks for *Ysu*. The barman tells him they don't stock drinks like that.

'D'you mean Northern drinks?'

The barman stares at him, then asks him to leave. Andrews walks out into the square and stands in the middle, in front of a broken fountain. He takes the flute box out of his pocket. The rain splashes onto the cloth as he opens the box, then he picks out the blackwood sections and pushes them together. He closes his eyes and raises the flute to his lips. His mouth makes the shape, and holds it: a perfect embouchure. He blows, and a shrill note rings around the small square. He opens his eyes again. A group in a doorway stop their conversation and glance across. He blows again, and now he is playing. He blows harder and the wood begins to warm and hum. The men in the doorways are coming out and walking towards him. He stares at them over the flute. His lip and his fingers are steady and sure.

He is playing an old song, a song he learnt from his father-in-law when he was courting Alicia. Its words are about a young man who has to leave his lover to go off to war. It is beautiful lament. Those are its words, but its words are not its meaning.

XXXV

The Bleaks were bleaker than ever. Bleaker, but more beautiful. Jude had flown straight over them this time, and down across the border heading back south. She could have claimed an overnight for such a long flight, but she didn't want to spend the night in a cheap hotel. She wanted to be back in the sky again, tired or no.

The mountains are giving way to trees and water as the South opens up ahead of her. The skies have cleared and the moonlight is cast across the landscape. Now she is over the lakes, and thinking again of her childhood and family holidays spent here. Her honeymoon was spent here too, but that was interrupted by the war. They had been foolhardy coming here for a honeymoon at the height of it all. What did they think? That the rockets would stop just because they were newlyweds?

On their wedding night in a lakeside cabin, a stray rocket from across the border hit the village across the lake. They were woken by the noise, and by the blaze of it through their curtains. Her new husband had dressed, told her she had to stay in the cabin to be safe, and set off in the car to help the villagers. He got back the following lunchtime, and wouldn't say a word to her for the rest of the week.

Only years later did she find out what he helped the villagers to do, how they smashed up a bakery run by four Northern brothers in the village, then rounded up the brothers and baked them in their own bread oven. He said they were spies, and that in any case he hadn't taken part in the lynching. He won't denounce it though, always insisting that the rocket came first, and everything that followed took place amid the fog of war. She thinks about it every day, but she doesn't talk to Tom about it. Not any more.

Jude flies with the radio switched off. She doesn't want the constant hiss and fuzz of interference and interruptions from men too stupid to fly for themselves, asking her if she is all right. The lakes look luminous below, metallic and magnetic.

Speed bonny boat like a bird on the wing

It's the boy. How can it be the boy? He's gone. He's dead. Perhaps when the cool box lid was open, some of his breath, some of his voice escaped into the plane? Does it rise to the ceiling like smoke? If it's in the air, then maybe she can breathe it in, maybe she has taken his voice deep into her own lungs, so now her inner voice contains his. Now her breath is interwoven with his breath. Everything she sings now is a duet.

Over the sea to Skye

If they ask her whether she opened the box she will deny it. After all, it was a long flight. If the seal on the cool box wasn't perfect, it could easily have compromised the temperature. A slight melt at the top of the ice. Nothing more. Nothing that would damage the lung, because the ice around the lung was still intact. It will be fine. She did her job and she made good time. It will be fine.

The sky is clear ahead and it feels good to be flying south again. Why? Why should it feel good to be going back to Tom, to be going back to all that?

Because of me. Because of us of course

Because of Jess. She thinks of her sister waking from her sleepwalk, coming home cold but unharmed. She pictures Jess smiling at her sister, at Jude, at the one person who never gave up hope, who never accepted that missing must mean dead. She pictures Jess with her arms wide open. Missing means being missed, that's all.

Speed bonny boat, like a bird on the wing

A Civil War in Nine Cigarettes:

9

The one found in his mother's coat pocket two weeks after she was killed in a rocket attack on the city. The boy took it up to his bedroom, opened the window and lit the cigarette with a match. The sky was quiet, still. From his attic room he could see out across the mews and over rows of roofs towards the spire of the cathedral. How had that huge edifice survived, and his mother not? What now separated him from his mother? Some solidity, some clotting of the air, the light, the smoke? He felt he could as easily disperse as gather.

Armistice. It could not bring her back. In the distance, parts of the city were smoking. All those fires would take months to put out. From now on he would carry his mother with him. He would breathe in her smoke and take her with him everywhere. He thought about that freakish story on the news about a boy who had absorbed his twin into his own body in the womb. As the boy grew up his twin lay curled inside him, lifeless and curled like a foetus. Until the doctors found it and cut it out the boy and his twin coexisted perfectly, secretly. So it would be with his mother. He would breathe in her spirit and never let it out.

He hadn't smoked before and it was making him choke, so he held the cigarette out of the window between drags and watched the smoke curl away. He imagined the smoke inside him curling into a chimera, his twin, his mother.

XXXVI

Baras wakes and the fruit fly is still there, looping in front of his eyes, obsessed with him. He has no energy to swat it away. He is back in the elegant room, with its polished table and a new bowl of mixed fruit. A vase of flowers half obscures the window. He doesn't know what time it is, nor how long he has been unconscious. All he knows is that there is some light through the window, the beginning or end of a day.

The minister is sitting by his bed. He is wired and tubed and seems to be plugged in to various machines with digits flashing alongside him. His chest is painful, but he is alive. He shifts his limbs under the bedclothes. He is intact. No, he is more than intact, because he has a new lung. Even now, the air feels thicker, richer. Double cream. Triple cream. His new lung is stronger, better able to draw the breath of life. He has not been crucified.

The minister sees his eyes open. She smiles and leans forward, tilting her head to face him.

'Welcome back.'

He would like to reply. He would like to thank her for being here when he came back. He would like to use this new breath to tell her everything he couldn't say before. Then she would understand. Then she would give him what he needs. But just now all he can do is lie here. A nurse leans over from the other side of his bed and starts checking his tubes and wires.

'Can he hear me?' the minister asks the nurse. 'He's not responding.'

'Maybe he can, maybe he can't. It'll be a while before he can give a response.'

The minister leans over and looks into his eyes, but it reminds him of the surgeon before the operation, so he shuts his eyes again.

'Is it a good sign that he can open his eyes?'

The nurse lifts his wrist from the bed and takes his pulse. She replies to the minister without looking up.

'It's a major operation. And the lung was not perfect.'

'That's why he had it swapped, surely?'

'Not the old lung, the new one. It came a long way and didn't travel well.'

Baras thinks of wine. He imagines a mouth full of wine that travelled very well indeed. He thinks of sitting outside his house in the mountains, under the trees with a glass of dark red wine. He looks into the glass and the wine is swirling, getting darker. Darker and thicker.

'Can I do anything to help? To improve his chances?'

The nurse lays Baras' arm gently back on the bed, and swats at the fruit fly circling above him.

'Just stay with him. And pray for him. Do you still do that?'

The nurse looks at the minister for the first time, and smiles.

'Yes', says the minister. 'We still do that.'

The nurse leaves the room, and Baras opens his

eyes again. The minister stands up and holds both hands out in front of her, clenched into fists.

'I have a new trick for you.'

She smiles, and opens the hands to reveal two pawns from the marble chess set, one from each side – red and blue.

'Now watch this.'

She closes her fists and knocks them together. When she opens them the red and blue pawns have swapped hands. She can see his eyes widen, and she thinks she sees a light return to them. She closes her hands again and lifts them together in front of her face, like a desperate prayer. She blows twice into the hands, as if she's trying to clear some sand stuck between her fingers. Then she slowly opens them and the pawns have vanished.

ACKNOWLEDGEMENTS

Acknowledgements are due to Victoira Adderley, Stephen Benson, Anthony McCluskey and Dermot Rafferty for background material. My thanks also to my editor Robin Robertson, Ellah Allfrey, and my agent David Godwin. As ever, my love and thanks to Ruth, Joe, Paddy and Griff.